A DARK ENCHANTMENT

Recent Titles by Margaret Pemberton from Severn House

A DARK ENCHANTMENT

Margaret Pemberton

This title first published in Great Britain 2001 by
SEVERN HOUSE PUBLISHERS LTD of
9–15 High Street, Sutton, Surrey SM1 1DF.
Originally published 1979 in Great Britain under the
title of *The Guilty Secret*.
This title first published in the USA 2001 by
SEVERN HOUSE PUBLISHERS INC of
595 Madison Avenue, New York, N.Y. 10022.

British Library Cataloguing in Publication Data

Pemberton, Margaret
   A dark enchantment
   1.   Portugal - Fiction
   2.   Love stories
   I.   Title
   823.9'14 [F]

   ISBN 0-7278-5769-X

Printed and bound in Great Britain by
MPG Books Ltd., Bodmin, Cornwall.

*For my sister Janet
and her husband David.*

One

The face looking back at me from the mirror didn't look like the face of a woman who had killed two people, one of them a child of eight.

Titian-red hair hung silkily to my shoulders framing an oval face with straight nose and green eyes. It was a face that had given me no shortage of admirers, and it was a face I could barely look at. Quickly I turned from the mirror, fighting down a familiar wave of panic. It was over. All over. I had to start life afresh. Forget the past and think about the future.

Below me lay the breathtaking panorama of Viana Do Castelo and the Portuguese coastline as it curved hazily southwards towards Ofir. I pushed the thought of Ofir away from me. I wasn't ready for it yet. I needed another few days of seclusion. A breathing space before I put on my mask of normality and was enclosed amid the bosom of family and friends. Seeing again the compassion in their eyes. The careful skirting around the subject uppermost in their minds. Catching them unawares, when the compassion changed to blatant curiosity and it was only too easy to read their thoughts. How did I really feel? What

was it like to kill two people? No. I wasn't ready for that
yet. Sometimes I doubted if I ever would be.

I had been holed up in the Edwardian grandeur of the
Hotel De Santa Luzia for over a week. As a refuge it was
ideal. It was perched one thousand feet high overlooking the
Igreja Santa Luzia, an imposing religious monument I had
not had the energy to enter. Far below lay the town. That
too, was still unexplored. It was early in the season and the
Hotel had only a handful of guests. I liked it that way. I
liked the fact that it was so inaccessible that casual callers
didn't stop off on their way to places further north or
further south. For the first time in nearly a year I was no
longer the object of curious eyes and I was in no hurry to
reach Ofir. Perhaps in another week ...

There was a soft knock and I walked quickly across the
thickly carpeted bedroom, opening the door to the maid
who had brought me coffee. She smiled. If the English girl
wished to spend the days in her room it was no concern of
hers.

I took the tray over to the small terrace and sipped it,
wishing it was eight-o-clock and not six, and that I could
take my tablets and go to bed. The tablets were my life-
saver. They ensured a deep, dreamless stupor instead of
the nightmares that left me waking with cries of terror, the
sweat pouring off me, re-living again my own private hell.

I finished the coffee and lay down on the bed. If only it
were possible to go back in time. How often had I wished
that? Every day? Every hour? To go back to the night of
Phil's party and the bright lights and the gaiety and
laughter. To go back and stay there. Not to walk out into the
darkness ... It had been a good party. Phil's parties always
were. Rozalinda was radiant, her ears and throat glittering
with diamonds, Harold watching her with slavish devotion.

Rozalinda, our mutual Aunt Harriet had remarked, had been lucky in life. Strange that Rozalinda had been the one to be a success, when as children I had always been the lucky one. Though she hadn't been Rozalinda then. Rose Lucas and as prone to tantrums then as she was now. Though now, an internationally known film star and married to a millionaire, she could afford to have tantrums. When we were children Phil had always said brutally:

"When you've stopped screaming and shouting *then* you can play. You can't have it all your own way *all* the time."

But she had. At sixteen she was modelling. At seventeen she was doing television commercials. At eighteen she had her first small film part. At twenty she was a star, and at twenty-three she had married the doting Harold, who had at least a million pounds to his credit and if Phil was to be believed, considerably more.

It was Harold's money that had bought Rozalinda what she called her 'Enclave' at Ofir. A cluster of luxurious villas for herself and friends and family, set among pinewoods and only yards from what Rozalinda claimed was the most spectacular beach in Europe. There was no fishing village full of Portuguese locals to spoil Rozalinda's private paradise. Only a couple of hotels that she managed to turn a blind eye to. Harold had tried unsuccessfully to buy them out but the Portuguese government had put an end to that little scheme. However, he had been more successful where the owners of the private villas were concerned. Rozalinda had, as usual, got her own way. The 'Enclave' was as private and exclusive as money could buy. Aunt Harriet spent most of the year there. As yet I had never been. I closed my eyes. Rozalinda was spoilt, but she had shown unexpected depths during the hellish months leading up to the trial and the ensuing nightmare after. Even Phil had admitted that she wasn't as self-centred as he had always supposed. It was her money that had paid my fare to Portugal, offering me the use of one of the villas for as long as I cared to stay. Aunt Harriet was already there and awaiting my arrival. I knew that my dalliance in Viana could only be causing her concern. Dear Aunt Harriet. Always there when needed. Loved by all of us. For Rozalinda and myself she was our Great-Aunt, never fussing over us like our parents did. Always treating us as grown-ups. For Phil she was even more important. His parents had died when he was thirteen and it was Aunt Harriet, no relation at all, who took him into her home, paying for his piano lessons, seeing to it that he had the best teachers that money could buy. When a neighbour had asked her why she spent so much time and money on the child of people who had been comparative strangers to her, she had replied tersely:

"The boy is brilliant."

For Aunt Harriet that was enough. She was right of course. Phil *was* brilliant. It was ironic that so far, all his years of study had brought him little renown, whereas Rozalinda's face smiled languidly down from cinema hoardings the world over. He played publicly a couple of times a month, the rest of his time spent in teaching, eked out by two days a week at a local school where he taught not only music, but English and Maths and more often than not found himself with a whistle round his neck surrounded by grubby schoolboys on the sports field. As an actress on the stage, Rozalinda had no real talent, only on film did she spring to life with devastating effect. By rights the fame that was hers should have been Phil's. At least that was my opinion. I wondered if it was Phil's as well. If it was he showed no signs of it. The only thing he ever said, was that they had got the wrong girl. That I was the beauty, not Rozalinda. But if I was, I wasn't sufficiently aware of it. I had done what I had always wanted to do. Become a nurse.

My thoughts were straying along paths that were becoming too painful. I thought instead of Mary Collins, or Farrar as she now was. Mary had made up the quartet of our childhood and Mary was going to be at Ofir as well. It would be good to see her again. Mary's steady grey eyes would hold no pity or curiosity, just the love born of a friendship twenty years old. As children the four of us had lived in Templar's Way, a small village perched precariously on the edge of the North Downs in Kent. My father had been the family doctor, Mary's the village greengrocer. As children it was Mary who was the peacemaker of our squabbles. Mary who persuaded Phil to let Rozalinda come along with us on our expeditions, even when her selfishness threatened to wreck Phil's carefully laid plans for a battle of cowboys and indians in the nearby woods. Rozalinda never would take her turn at being a cowboy. She always wanted the painted face and feathers. I smiled affectionately. She had certainly got them now.

Mary's placidity and gentleness had been the saving of our quartet. Phil always wanted to leave Rozalinda behind and then she would go crying to Aunt Harriet and both Phil and myself would be in disgrace for not being kind to her. I wondered if Rozalinda ever realised what a lot she had owed Mary as a child. She probably did because the friendship between them had outlasted childhood, and though no two life-styles could be as different as Rozalinda's and Mary's, they were still close. In fact Rozalinda had said herself that the next few weeks at the Enclave would be just like old times. The four of us all together again, for she had even persuaded Phil to fly out and join us for a few weeks, luring him with the promise of a quiet room and grand piano on which to practice.

Mary's husband, Tom, would be there too. He had come as rather a surprise. Mary was such a plain and quiet person that no-one had expected her to marry anyone as outstandingly handsome as Tom Farrar. But Tom Farrar had chosen well. Mary's life revolved around him and their two young children and if ever a man was adored, he was. The rest of us visited them at irregular intervals, finding in Mary's peaceful home the rest and solace we missed in our own lives. This would be the first holiday that Mary and Tom had taken away from the children and I wondered how Mary was surviving it. She would be like a mother hen without its chicks, but Great Aunt Harriet had been adamant that she needed the rest.

"That girl is ageing prematurely," she had said to me over the telephone whilst persuading me that I, too, needed a complete rest. "It will do both of you the world of good to spend a few weeks down here in the sunshine."

It was the thought of Mary's companionship that had decided me. That and the faint worry that Aunt Harriet's words had left. What could be causing Mary so much anxiety that it was ageing her prematurely? Aunt Harriet wasn't prone to exaggeration. I wondered if it was Tom and then dismissed the idea. No-one could possibly be unhappy married to Mary. She'd obviously been overworking and of course the trial and its aftermath had left its mark on her as it had everyone else close to me. It would be a long time before I forgot the agony on Phil's face. As for Aunt Harriet's ... I reached for my handbag and tablets. I could wait no longer for the oblivion they brought. If I could have slept through the day as well as the night I would gratefully have done so.

The sinking rays of the sun filled the room with smokey light. In coming away I had intended to determine my future. So far it was as hazy as ever. I could never go back to St Thomas's and nursing. The thought of a new job, of interviews, of explaining away the gap in my life that the trial had left was too daunting an ordeal. There was always Phil's alternative. The tablets were already beginning to work and I felt my stomach muscles slowly relaxing, my eyes gently closing. Phil had recently asked me to marry him. Drowsily I thought of marriage to Phil. It would be a pleasant existence. We had always been together. Phil was insistent that we always should be together. We wouldn't have much money, but I didn't care about that. Besides, we would have a home. The cottage in Templars Way that Phil's parents had left to him, and he had a brilliant future. He was only twenty-four ...

The only marriages I had seen at close quarters had been Mary's and Rozalinda's. Neither of them had encouraged me to take the same step. True, Mary was happy, but I knew that I could never be at someone else's beck and call as Mary was at Tom's. All that mattered to Mary was that Tom was happy, no matter what her own wishes and desires were. It seemed to me rather an unequal arrangement. As for Harold and Rozalinda ... There it was completely the other way round. Harold's eyes followed Rozalinda's every move with dog-like devotion. And I knew Rozalinda well enough to know that without his money Harold wouldn't last a day. He hadn't earned his million for himself but had inherited it, and though he was kind and pleasant, he was also a rather stupid man who had even on occasions managed to bore the patient Mary. No, Rozalinda's marriage was no encouragement to anyone. There had been gossip some months back that Rozalinda was having an affair with her latest leading man. Gossip that

Harold's public relations man had been quick to squash. Still, it was news that would have surprised no-one who knew her. The thought of Rozalinda being a faithful wife needed a definite effort of imagination. And that she should be faithful to Harold, who was thirty years older than her and who had nothing to offer in the way of looks or personality, seemed downright improbable. But Rozalinda was careful. She had planned her own career with alarming single-mindedness. She wouldn't lose Harold and his millions for a passing love affair, no matter how handsome the face. When we had been in our teens it had been Phil who had been the centre of her attention. I'd often wondered if, had she not left Templar's Way when she did, she would finally have wormed her way into his affections. She had made no secret of the fact that she wanted him, and what Rozalinda wanted she usually got. Phil had been totally immune to her advances. He didn't even seem aware of them. His sole preoccupation was his music. If there were two sexes, Phil had shown no knowledge of the fact. Then had come the film parts and Rozalinda had left the village, moving out of our orbit and into the more exciting world of Harold's. Yet even now, whenever she looked at Phil there was something in her eyes that I couldn't quite define. I imagine he was the only man Rozalinda had ever wanted and failed to get. A perpetual challenge to her self esteem. I only hoped she didn't try to rectify the situation when Phil reached Ofir. Rozalinda might be a sex symbol to the Western world, but to Phil she was Rose Lucas who whined when she didn't get her own way and had no appreciation of his musical talents. They were friends, and only friends and Phil wouldn't hesitate to tell her so. Tact wasn't one of his qualities and after the unadulterated adoration she was used to, I imagined any home truths from Phil would be very ill received.

Sleep was beginning to drift over me in waves. Aunt Harriet would be happy if I married Phil. Phil would be happy too. Perhaps Phil was right. Perhaps we should get married.

With none of the past men in my life had I felt so at ease as with him. I came round to full consciousness with a rush of realisation. I was mad! How could I think of marriage after what had happened? How could I contemplate marriage to anyone? I covered my face with my hands, and for the hundredth time began to cry myself to sleep.

Two

I heard his car early the next morning. I was sitting beneath the scarlet awning that shaded my bedroom terrace, eating warm rolls and grateful for the strong coffee that cleared my mouth of the stale taste the tablets left, when there came the high pitched whine of a car engine beginning the twisting ascent to the hotel. For several minutes I listened as he changed gears, the tree shadowed bends twisting with increasing steepness. Through the heavy foliage I caught my first glimpse of the car. It was a Lamborgini with a GB plate and at the speed he was driving I was glad the hotel was so sparsely inhabited he was unlikely to meet anyone coming in the opposite direction. The road curved round to the rear of the hotel and the main entrance so that I was unable to get a glimpse of the driver, but when I went down to reception a little while later to telephone Aunt Harriet and put her mind at rest as to where I was, I saw him clearly. The large, sunny dining-room had only three occupants. Two of them German businessmen who had arrived two days earlier. The third the Lamborgini's driver. My brief glance told me he was somewhere in his late twenties, with the most amazing shock of sun-gold hair I had ever seen on a grown man. He glanced upwards and I hurriedly averted my eyes, walking quickly across the marbled entrance hall towards the telephone, but not before I had seen a disturbingly attractive face with strong jawline and hazel eyes. It was the eyes that held my attention as I struggled to get through to Ofir and Aunt Harriet. There was something familiar about them yet I hadn't seen him before ...

Aunt Harriet was understanding but brisk:

"You *did* hire a car, didn't you?"

"Yes, I've no transport problems."

That was part of the therapy recommended by my psychiatrist. One of the ways in which he thought I could regain self-confidence and emotional stability. I hadn't the heart to disillusion him.

"That's good. It's only half an hour's drive down here from Viana, but for goodness sake be careful of the cows."

"Cows? It's the main motorway south. What do I need to be careful of cows for?"

"Because the motorway is a deteriorated Roman road, with the added benefit of being like India. Cows are everywhere. Side of the road. Middle of the road and they've no traffic sense. Tranquil creatures, cows ..."

"Yes Aunt Harriet," I interrupted before she got too side-tracked onto bovine virtues. "I'll be with you in another few days. I just thought I'd do a little sight-seeing up here first."

"Well, if you're sure that's the only reason for your delay." Aunt Harriet didn't sound sure but then she knew me very well. "Mary and Tom are here *and* Rozalinda and Harold. I'll tell them you'll be here later this week."

"Yes, do that. And take care of yourself."

"Bye, God bless." Aunt Harriet said as I slowly put down the receiver.

I knew now why those hazel eyes had looked so familiar. The colour was different, but the expression in them was identical to that in my own. They were the eyes of someone who had suffered and had built a wall around themselves. From the very first I knew that the golden-haired Englishman was seeking sanctuary in the same manner I was.

Idly I swung the stand of picture postcards round, finally selecting one that showed the Hotel, the small red canopies that fluttered over its balconies giving it an air of nineteen-thirtyish grandeur. Carefully I wrote the name of Doctor McClure and the address of the psychiatric clinic I had just been discharged from, then I stopped, staring at the blank space for the messages. What did one write to a man who had been alternately kind and cruel, patient and furious in his efforts to get me back to so called normality?

Wish you were here? Hardly.

Having a lovely time? I could imagine his comments to that.

In the end I simply scrawled 'Jenny' in large letters across the space, and handed it over to the dark eyed boy on reception to post. For the first time since I had booked into the Santa Luzia I did not return immediately to my room. Doctor McClure *had* instilled some confidence into me. I might have found some of his forms of therapy futile but I was certainly in far better shape when I had left the clinic than when I had entered. For that I had to give him some credit. My daily retreats into my room, locked with myself and my memories, spending whole days at a time in brooding, was the most dangerous thing I could do if I wanted to recover fully. McClure had been adamant.

"Get a car. Meet people. Work. Travel. Open your mind to fresh experiences. Have an affair. Anything. But don't creep into the haven of your bed each day. You'll only slip backwards, Jenny."

Since I'd left the clinic I'd done exactly that. The only positive thing I had done was to hire the car, and if a quick uninterested drive through France and Northern Spain could be called travel, then I had travelled. But not in the way Doctor McClure had meant. Not with my senses open to fresh experiences. Not with any anticipation of enjoyment. Well, I wasn't prepared to follow all his advice. I wasn't going to go back to work as yet. And having an affair wasn't exactly as easy to do as hiring a car. Besides, affairs meant confidences shared, past experiences recounted. I definitely wasn't playing that game with anybody. It was bad enough friends knowing about me. I wasn't going to broadcast the news to any new man who should walk across my path. But I could travel in the way McClure had meant. Become a tourist instead of a hermit. I took a steadying breath and went out into the hotel grounds to the car.

I took the winding road, drenched in the overhang of greenery, far more slowly than the Englishman had. For a brief moment the car swung out of the trees and onto the small promenade that fronted the Igreja Santa Luzia and gave photographic enthusiasts a one hundred and eighty degree view of the Portuguese coastline and the valley of the river Lima. A couple of cars were already parked. I swept past them diving down once more into cool greenness, the road curving snakelike till it emerged onto the main road into Viana. Minutes later I was parked in the main square, looking every inch the typical English tourist. It was an easy accomplishment. The rest of the female population dressed completely in black, shawls over their heads as they chattered loudly, their baskets of shopping over their arms, or more usually, piles of washing or sacks of grain carried with ease on their heads. Certainly a fresh experience. I selected a reasonably clean looking street cafe and ordered coffee, sitting out on the pavement and watching this totally new world go by.

On the street corner nearest to me, a cheerful, middle-aged woman wearing knee length socks and wooden clogs was selling fish from a barrow. This entailed a lot of gesticulating and loud laughter with her customers and a lot of nods in my direction and then more chatter and the words "Inglese". It seemed I was one of the first tourists of the year and though I didn't look wealthy would probably spend a lot of money in the shops around the square. Most of the shops' stock seemed to be displayed outside the premises. Pots and pans, gaily decorated pottery, hand knitted sweaters and brightly coloured rugs hung from doorways and walls, was spread out on the pavement. Around the ornate fountain a group of men gathered, deep in conversation, occasionally spitting with great gusto, hands thrust into their baggy trouser pockets as their women folk scurried up and down on the square with huge weights on their heads, their hands free to grasp at straying toddlers. The Lamborgini came as I knew it would, skidding to a halt amidst a cloud of dust on the far side of the square. He slammed the car door shut, locking it and then looking around him without much interest. He was tall and slim, and when he finally moved, it was with loose limbed grace but there was nothing effeminate about him. Rather the opposite. He gave the impression of strength and aggression being held on a very tight chain. The men at the fountain turned to watch him as he strolled slowly along past the shops with their profusion of goods and souvenirs then they turned back into their tight little group, muttering. I could well imagine what they were saying. The tourist was not a man to pick a fight with. There were no smiles from them as he passed closely, though the women smiled, but then I imagined that most women would. He was the sort of man by whom any female, sophisticate or peasant, would like to be noticed. He disappeared into the dark depths of a cafe on the far side of the square, emerging minutes later with a bottle of wine and a glass. He sat at one of the deserted metal tables, leaning back easily on his chair, pouring what looked like a tumblerfull of wine.

I watched intrigued. Was the stranger's great secret to be nothing more interesting than alcoholism? Somehow I doubted it. He looked like a man who had himself very firmly under control. My presence, even at the distance across the cobbled square must have been obvious to him, but he didn't look my way. I didn't have to be vain to know that I was a girl men stopped twice to look at. My problem in life had been fighting off unwanted admirers, not encouraging them. But as far as the Englishman was concerned I didn't rate a second glance. And he knew I was staying at the same hotel, and from my colouring it must be equally apparent that we were the same nationality. Despite myself, I felt interested. I ordered another coffee, settling myself comfortably in the warmth of the morning sun, letting my imagination run over the list of possibilities that caused his eyes to hold the same deadened expression mine did.

It wasn't till eleven-o-clock when he paid the waiter and rose languidly to his feet and back to his car, that I realised for the first time in months my mind had been totally occupied by something other than my own nightmare, and all due to curiosity about a man I hadn't even spoken to as yet. Perhaps Doctor McClure's therapy was working.

Three

I didn't return directly to my own car, but strolled aimlessly through the narrow back streets, small doorways opening onto dark interiors of wine filled shelves and bags of wheat and dried beans. There were plenty of pastry shops, their windows crammed with delicious sugar encrusted buns and cakes. I ventured in, pointing out two and watching intrigued as the smiling woman behind the counter parcelled them expertly into a neat package. She had wasted her time. Once out in the sun again I undid the neat folds of stiff paper, eating as I strolled along. A group of children giggled at my approach, scurrying into a doorway until I had passed by. A toothless old woman, shawl clutched tightly around her head, waved her stick at them, shouting chastisement. I smiled and walked on, dodging beneath lines of spotless washing that hung across from house to house, seeking my leisurely way back to the square.

I felt better than I had done for a long time. The fresh air had revitalised me. Tomorrow, I decided, I would go further north and take my camera with me. Being a tourist wasn't such painful therapy after all.

As I entered the dining-room he was just about to leave. He placed his napkin on the side of his table and rose to his feet, his eyes meeting mine as he did so. This time I didn't avert my head. I couldn't. Our eyes held, the feeling of physical attraction so strong that it seemed ridiculous I should be making my way to my own table and not to his. He stood quite still, his chair pushed back, his fingertips resting lightly on the white cloth in front of him. There was no hint of a smile on the firm sensuous mouth, and the expression in his eyes was unreadable, yet the magnetism was so strong I was unable to move. Manuel, the head waiter, hurried over to me, carefully ushering me to my table, breaking the spell. The Englishman's eyes dropped. As I sat down I saw him nod briefly in Manuel's direction, leaving the room without a backward glance.

Over the past few months I had grown quite accustomed to knots of painful tension in my stomach. Now a new feeling was forming there. One of suppressed excitement. I stirred rice and eggs and sauce meditatively around my plate. Was it just the feeling that we were two of a kind, both alone and desperately unhappy. Or was that only my imagination. Nothing more than wishful thinking. Even worse, was I subconsciously on the look out for McClure's other suggestion of therapy. A new love affair. A carefree association with someone who knew nothing about my past and whom I would have no reason to tell? I cast the thought aside. For one thing, I doubted that any involvement with the Englishman would be carefree. Intense. Distressing. But never carefree. I wondered how long he was staying at the Santa Luzia. When Manuel came to remove my plate I asked casually:—

"Is your new guest English as well?"

A smile flashed across Manuel's dark face. "Yes. Senor

Brown is here until the end of the week."

I smiled noncommittally and asked if they had any of the cheese I had had last night for dessert. Only too anxious to please, Manuel pushed the sweet trolley, heavy with cream rolls and flans, to one side and hurried off to find the cheese.

Brown. It wasn't the kind of name that I had expected. I spent the afternoon on the terrace soaking up the sunshine and looking out over the swaying sea of trees to the distant sea. I had a book in my hand, but my thoughts kept drifting away from it and onto the more interesting subject of Mr Brown. What gave his eyes that frightening expression I had grown so used to whenever I looked in a mirror? I determined to find out that night after dinner.

I judged eight-o-clock to be about the right time to make my entrance. Manuel's eyes opened wide at my approach. Previously I hadn't bothered to change for dinner. Tonight I had gone to town. My dress was deceptively simple, Chiffon, the exact shade of my eyes, that hung closely around my breasts and hips, swirling softly into a flared skirt. I had spent more time than usual on my face and hair, spraying perfume at wrists and throat, gold earrings swinging gently against the red of my hair. If I didn't lure him into conversation tonight, I might as well abandon all hope. I sensed him rather than saw him. Sensed also the turned heads of the businessmen and the murmur of appreciation from a table full of early season tourists. To Rozalinda, admiration was meat and drink. Under normal circumstances I would hardly have been aware of it. But tonight, like Rozalinda, I was going out of my way to be noticed. Carefully I kept my eyes away from his table, ordering my dinner, surprising Manuel by asking for half a bottle of Viana Verde instead of my usual mineral water. Through the draped windows could be seen the distant

mountains that separated Portugal from Spain, turning a
hazy grey beneath a sky of flame. I heard his chair move
back and continued to eat leisurely. I had no intention of
making the first move. If he had no desire to talk to me that
was fine by me. True, I would be disappointed. I couldn't
remember ever before having to *try* to fall into conversation
with a desirable male, and there *is* such a thing as pride.
Rozalinda would have been quite direct in her approach,
but I wasn't Rozalinda and didn't want to be. Before my
own private nightmare had distorted my life Aunt Harriet
had said I was too shy and retiring. But eighteen months
with Doctor McClure in the psychiatric clinic had changed
me radically. My personality would never be the same
again, and I was just beginning to come to terms with the
new Jennifer Harland.

Unhurriedly I finished the delicious local wine, watching
as the candy-floss clouds deepened from flame to purple,
and then casually I walked into the bar.

The bar was the only room of even slightly modern decor
in the Santa Luzia. All the rooms had a carefully tended
Edwardian elegance, emphasized even more so on an
evening when the massive chandeliers glittered with a
hundred lights. The bar was a cosy room decorated entirely
in a glowing crimson. Carpet, walls, ceiling and curtains
met in a single blend of colour. The soft leather seats that
ran around two sides of the small room were in black
leather. So too were the plushly topped bar stools.
Everything else, the solid looking foot rest that skirted the
bar, the fitments, were all in heavy gilt. Whether the effect
strived for was modern or Victorian was hard to make out.
The result was one of warmth and comfort. The two
businessmen paused in their conversation as I entered. The
young barman beamed. The Englishman, sat at the far

curve of the bar on a bar stool, nursing a glass in his hand, didn't look up. I sat some distance from him and ordered a vodka and tonic, I didn't normally drink and what the effect the vodka would have on top of the wine and my tablets was anyone's guess.

My drink came and with it some admiring bantering from the barman. I smiled but did not get involved. It was the Englishman I wished to talk to. Perhaps ordering the vodka had been a bad move. Perhaps he was only interested in respectable girls who did not sit in bars, even five class hotel bars. A sensation of heat flooded through me. He had lifted his head from his glass and was looking at me. With immense effort I kept my eyes lowered. He ordered another drink for himself. A scotch on the rocks, but still I knew he was looking at me. When I had stood it as long as I could I raised my head, forgetting my previous intentions and said:–

"It's very quiet for this time of the year, isn't it?"

His eyes met mine with devastating effect.

"Yes. Rather like an elegant mausoleum."

"In another month it will be packed to capacity and this little bar will be crammed with tourists."

This time he smiled, but the reserve was still there. The eyes still devoid of any true expression, carefully masked so that the suffering in them should not be exposed to the rest of the curious world. It was a trick I had learnt myself very successfully.

"Will you still be here when it is?"

"No. I'm leaving at the end of the week."

"Would you like another of those?" he nodded in the direction of my empty glass."

"No thank you. Could I have a fruit juice please?"

"One orange and another scotch, he said to the waiter,

slipping down from his stool and moving to the one next to me.

A current ran between us, so sharp and vibrant that I knew he was conscious of it himself. He had to be.

"Are you alone?" he asked, passing me my drink, scooping ice into his glass.

"Yes."

He raised his glass to mine. "That makes two of us. Didn't your mother tell you never to talk to strangers?"

"I don't. Usually."

He stared into his glass, swirling the chunks of ice around broodingly. "I have a feeling I should say nice to have met you and bid you a hasty goodnight."

My heart was beating painfully. "And?"

"Against my better judgement I'm not going to." The harsh lines around his mouth softened slightly and again there was a hint of a smile. "What is your name?"

"Jenny."

"Do you smoke, Jenny?"

"Not often. I will now."

He lit two cigarettes and passed one to me, our fingers touching as he did so. It was as if sparks struck between us. If you go near the fire you'll only get burned, I said silently to myself. Use your better judgement. Wish him a short, sharp goodnight and go to bed.

He said :– "I'm Jonathan."

I remained on the bar stool.

"I saw you in the square this morning."

"Why didn't you speak?" I managed at last.

He shrugged. "I'm not on the look out for a holiday romance. Are you?"

"No." It was true. I hadn't been on the look out for it. That it was already beginning to happen was neither here nor there.

"This is a hell of a place to come by yourself," he said.

"You came."

"I'm at least ten years older than you and looking for peace and quite. A friend told me this was the exact spot to find it."

"I'm not quite so sure about the ten years, but I wanted somewhere quiet too."

He said, and it wasn't a careless question, "Why?"

Here it was. The nitty gritty. To tell or not to tell. What had Doctor McClure said to me? It is unnecessary to torture yourself by reliving the past with every new acquaintance you make. Think of it as a form of egotism. Wanting to shock and be the centre of attention. That will soon stop you doing it. I made up my mind then and there.

"I'm recuperating from a nervous breakdown. I've just spent eighteen months in a private clinic."

"I'm sorry." The words weren't the polite ones so many others had given. He meant them. And he wouldn't probe. I breathed a sigh of relief. I had told him some of the truth, and what I had told him wouldn't affect whatever relationship lay ahead of us. Jonathan Brown wasn't the kind of man to fight shy of someone whose mental health had needed treatment anymore than he would have fought shy of someone whose physical health had needed treatment. I knew that instinctively.

"And you?" I asked. "Why did you want peace and quiet?"

Under the gentle glow of the wall lights his skin paled and the hand nursing his glass clenched so that the knuckles showed white.

"Sorry." I said hastily. "I shouldn't have asked."

"Why not? I asked you. Only my answer isn't so simple."

He didn't attempt to explain further and I was painfully aware that I had trodden on forbidden ground.

The sun-gold hair was thick, curling into the nape of his neck, falling across his forehead in an unruly wave. His skin was lightly tanned, as if he had spent several weeks further south. I had not been mistaken about the mouth either. It was strong and firm, with a sensual full underlip, the jawline clearly defined and hard.

His mood had changed with my question, his face taut and grim. I said lightly:– "This is the first time I've been to Portugal. I'm going further south at the end of the week. To Ofir."

I could almost see him come back from the past and into the present.

"Ofir. That's a beach resort isn't it?"

"Yes. A friend of mine owns several villas there."

"You don't look like one of the world weary rich."

I laughed. "I'm not. Just a poverty stricken hanger on."

The smile was back again, the tension gone. He was looking at my left hand. I said:– "I'm twenty-two and single."

"And a mind reader. I was only three years out. I'm twenty-nine."

He didn't tell me what I most wanted to know.

"When I leave here I'm going across the border to Vigo. I have friends there but I doubt if they are as wealthy as yours seem."

"It would be a little difficult," I smiled, thinking of Harold's millions and Rozalinda's Swiss bank accounts.

"Then until you leave for the lap of luxury perhaps we could do some sightseeing together?"

His hand brushed against mine as he reached for my empty glass, sending pins and needles down my spine. If I wanted to play safe all I had to say was no.

I said instead:– "I'd like that."

He ordered me another drink of orange. "What about Valenca? Have you been there yet?"

"No. It's near the Spanish frontier isn't it?"

He nodded. "On the river Minho. Oliveira, my friend in Vigo, told me not to miss it. Apparently it's the original medieval toy-town. Walls and ramparts all intact and mini church and houses squeezed inside. I think it will be a day to remember."

Hardly able to breathe for the excitement of his presence, I thought it would be too.

Four

The next day at breakfast he remained seated at his table in the far corner of the dining room, and I remained seated at mine. As I entered he lifted his head and the corners of his mouth lifted in a slight smile. I breathed a secret sigh of relief. He hadn't changed his mind then. Last night hadn't been a sudden impulse that he had regretted on waking. I was still only halfway through my rolls and coffee when he strolled past, saying quietly:–

"I'll meet you at reception in about fifteen minutes, OK?"

"OK," I nodded, a surge of happiness welling up inside me. It had been so long since I had experienced any feeling even remote to happiness that for a few choked filled seconds I thought I was actually going to cry. Fool, I said inwardly. Isn't it about time? Everyone said I would be happy again, I've just been too pig-headed to believe them. For months I had felt that I had no *right* to feel happiness. Not after what I had done. Doctor McClure had lost patience with me over that. He had been in turn both gentle and brutal, but always his message had been the same. Put the past behind me where it belonged. Nothing could change it. If I was to regain my mental and emotional stability then I had to start life afresh. Well, this morning McClure would have been pleased with me. While I waited for Jonathan I selected another postcard from the rack and wrote on it what had seemed so derisory only twenty-four hours ago. 'Having a lovely time, Jenny'. Then I addressed it to the clinic and handed it to the young boy who served on reception and didn't look a day over thirteen.

"Ready?"

I turned quickly, aware that my cheeks had flushed. "Yes. Camera, guide-book, map. Everything the well equipped tourist needs."

He grinned. "I think we can dispense with the map. There's only one road we can possibly take from Viana to Valenca. I don't think we risk getting lost.'"

"Maybe not, but there's wolves in those mountains and I'm not a girl to take chances."

"Now that I don't believe."

His hand reached for mine and we laughed.

"Not those sort of chances anyway."

Watched with interest by several of the Santa Luzia's army of staff we walked across the pink marbled hallway with its urns of trailing greenery and into the car park. That was the only sticky moment of the day.

"Yours or mine?" he asked, surveying both our neatly parked cars. "A Volkswagon is more sensible on these roads."

"And a Lamborgini more exciting."

"When my rear suspension goes I shall know who to blame," he said good-naturedly, opening the car door for me as I eased out a sigh of relief.

Even now, looking back on it, that day was magical. It was one of those special, sunny days that seem to occur only in childhood, when every single thing was fun and the sky was a permanent blue, and your companion and yourself were in perfect harmony. And like childhood I should have known from the start it was a perfection that couldn't last. We swooped down the first of the curves and onto the parapet fronting the religious monument that the Portuguese seemed to build on every available hill. Jonathan swerved to a halt.

"Have you seen that?"

At the foot of the granite steps leading up to the shrine stood an elderly, balding little man with a handkerchief tied rakishly around his neck. By his side was an object that looked as if it had escaped from a museum.

"What is it?"

"Only a genuine Zeiss Ikon box camera!" Jonathan said, reaching for his door handle. "It can't *work* surely! It must be some sort of con trick to get people to have their photographs taken. There must be a modern Instamatic inside. That thing must be at least fifty years old!"

I followed him round the front of the car to where the man, sensing custom, was straightening down the brilliant yellow cover that shielded his contraption from the sun, steadying the rickety tripod on which it perched.

"How much?" Jonathan asked.

The man delved into his pocket displaying four hundred escudos. Jonathan laughed, shaking his head, taking from his wallet one hundred and fifty escudos. The photographer looked suitably disappointed, and proffered three hundred escudos. Jonathan offered two hundred. A bargain had been struck, and the photographer beamingly placed us on the second of the steps, Jonathan's arms around my waist.

The photographer's head disappeared beneath the yellow drapery and then emerged almost immediately, making adjustments with a bit of rough wood that seemed to act as a light meter for him. Once more his head disappeared under the cloth his hands carefully inserted between slits.

"He isn't *really* going to take a photograph with that, is he?" I asked. "And how will we get it if he does? He'll have to send it to us."

Finally the balding head emerged and Jonathan stepped down to ask how we received the photograph, did he want our address?

The bald head shook vehemently. Lovingly he extricated a blank piece of card from the draped interior, dropping it into a solution of liquid that swirled in a narrow wooden box hanging at one end of his camera.

"I don't believe it," Jonathan said laughing. "It isn't a con. That thing is actually working and he's developing a negative!"

Unbelievingly we saw him lift the dripping, now dark piece of card, and position it carefully on a projection of wood in front of the camera's lens.

"What's he doing now?"

"Photographing the negative. This I just have to see to believe. Perhaps we should have given him the four hundred escudos he asked for. It would have been worth it for an experience like this!"

There was much dipping of our would be photograph in a bucket of solution and then, trimphantly he lifted from its murky depths, a photograph, slightly more grey and white than black and white, but a photograph, taken in five minutes flat with a camera that resembled those that waited to photograph a much early generation against the pyramids or with one foot triumphantly on a shot tiger. And not only *one* photograph, but two. Still wet, but showing two people, arms around each other, laughing into each other's eyes as if they were lovers. I wondered if the same thought struck Jonathan as he looked at his. If it did, he remained silent about it, saying only:–

"Get your camera from the car Jenny. If I don't photograph this fellow and his camera no-one is ever going to believe me!"

The photographer leant one arm proudly on his camera, the tripod swinging a trifle unsteadily, and beamed obligingly. Then we hurried into the car, the breeze, with nothing to stop it as it swirled in from the Atlantic, too chilly for comfort. As Jonathan swept round the curves of the steep hillside down into Viana I reflected that I was glad of seat belts, and that my nerves had certainly improved in the last few days.

Once on the narrow road north, Jonathan's driving slowed considerably. It had to. When a road is only twelve feet wide and oxen with horns with a five foot span amble down it, there is no alternative. The animals all looked well cared for, with glossy amber coats and ornate wooden harnesses. The old women or children leading them looked less well cared for, but all smiled as we slowed down, waiting till the oxen and the cart, usually full of hay and squealing toddlers had turned off into a farm track leaving the road clear again, or slowly easing round them, the children waving at us enthusiastically. Houses in delicate shades of pinks, greys and whites, their roofs the colour of deep peach, scattered the lush green fields and vines grew everywhere. Every cottage, no matter how humble, had its small piece of land and its vines.

"It all looks vaguely familiar," Jonathan said. "It reminds me of somewhere ..."

"Ireland. Ireland with vines and oranges and olives and almonds."

"And grapes. You're right, Jenny Wren. Though I've never seen the women in Ireland washing by the river banks as they do here."

"Another ten years and you probably won't see it here either. Though what disturbs me most about seeing them on their hands and knees pummelling the clothes on the rocks isn't the sheer hard work of it."

"No?"

"No. It's the fact that when they hang the washing out to dry or lay it on the boulders to dry, it's cleaner than mine is when it comes out of my automatic machine!"

He laughed. "So much for progress. Quick. Look at these three old women walking down the road dressed in black. They look like the original three witches!"

I smiled and waved and was rewarded by three toothless smiles as they hugged their shawls tighter around their bodies, gazing after the car in disbelief.

"I don't think Lamborgini's are exactly common round here."

"My dear Jenny," Jonathan said. "Lamborgini's are not common *anywhere*!" And again we were laughing. I was as much at ease in his company as I was in Phil's. With one important addition. Jonathan's body next to mine did things to my nervous system that Phil's could never have done. For the first time I was beginning to understand why Mary waited on Tom hand and foot. It was understandable if he had this effect on her, and if I could keep Jonathan by me, then I would move heaven and earth to do so.

"This is it," he said, waking me from my reverie. "Valenca."

I looked around in surprise. "It doesn't look medieval to me. It looks just like all the other little villages we've passed."

The road curved past a handful of houses with their inevitable washing hanging to dry in the sun, then, before we knew it we were out of it amid undulating green fields, the road narrowing alarmingly.

"We must have taken a wrong turn," I said as the track circled a green mound and wound steeply upwards. "We're going into somebody's back garden!"

Ahead of us lay an arched stone entrance, barely wide enough to allow a car through.

"Jonathan, stop! We're going to be in someone's house in a moment!"

He grinned. "I can't turn round here, there's nothing for it but to go ahead." With a surge the Lamborgini scraped through the momentary darkness of the ornate entrance and out again into brilliant sunshine. We drew in our breaths and stared.

"Well, I'll be damned," he said in amazement. "When Oliveira said it was a toytown he wasn't kidding."

Ahead of us the miniscule cobbled road swept on for a further few yards, steep banks of lush grass falling away at its sides. Then there was another stone arched entrance and through that could be seen a tantalising glimpse of Valenca. Cobbled streets crowded with barefoot children and chattering women, houses crammed together their frontages barely four feet wide. Slowly Jonathan edged the car through the massive protective gates and into Valenca's main street. As we parked the car among pleased stares, we felt like Gullivers. The church we had passed was like a model church. The square we parked in barely big enough to take the car. Everything had been cut down to fit within the medieval walls. The shops were obviously directed solely at the tourist trade, spilling over with cheap souvenirs and plastic effigies. A fat lady, comfortably seated beneath a gaily striped umbrella shouted gaily:–

"Frances?"

"No, Ingles," Jonathan shouted back with a smile. She beamed benevolently. Ingles was just as good. The Inglese would spend their money in Valenca just as the French and Germans did. She held out an apronful of apples and oranges, but Jonathan shook his head taking my arm and leading me down the sun-filled street. She smiled. By the time we returned, no doubt we would be grateful of an apple or an orange ...

We walked slowly, his arm pressing against mine, there was the usual pastry shop and we went inside, buying chocolate iced slabs of cake and sugared cream eclairs and a bottle of Viano Verde to wash it down with. Then, sharing a packet of sugared almonds, we browsed contentedly through the steep and narrow streets, turning unexpectedly into a mini courtyard ablaze with flowers, or listening to the strange sing-song of an elderly priest as he walked slowly across the cobbles, his cloak hardly moving in the still warmth, his head bent, his stick tapping out his way till he reached the door he wanted and stopped his hypnotic singing to knock gently.

Hand in hand we strolled towards the giant stone ramparts that circled the town. There were two encircling walls, and between them lay the undulating lush grass that grew in what had been a wide moat. Certainly the ancient inhabitants of Valenca had gone to extraordinary lengths to see that no raiding Spaniards from across the river invaded them. The sun was hot on our backs as we scrambled over the edge of the road that led from the outer entrance to the inner, gasping for breath as we plunged down the uneven ground to the grassy basin where only the bees hummed and an occasional dragonfly darted past on azure wings. I undid the neat paper package that held our pastries and Jonathan uncorked the wine and we passed the bottle one to the other as we hadn't had the forethought to bring paper cups and I was glad that we hadn't. With the last of the cakes eaten we leaned back against the comfort of the grassy bank, Jonathan's arm around my shoulders, and it seemed impossible that two days ago we hadn't even met.

"Happy?" Jonathan asked.

"Yes," I said. "I'm happy."

He smiled but I couldn't see his eyes from where I lay, my head crooked into his shoulder. More than anything I wanted to make Jonathan happy too. If there had come a moment for revealing my past, then those couple of hours spent in the idyll of Valenca's medieval walls, was the moment when I should have spoken. But to do so would have spoilt a perfect day. And I was too much of a coward. Not willing to risk my happiness in one fateful throw of the dice. Perhaps he would have been compassionate as others had been. But if not ... It was as if I couldn't face it. I would do what Doctor McClure had instructed. Leave the past where it belonged and think only of the present. I plucked idly at the grass, saying almost shyly:–

"Are you happy now, Jonathan?"

He didn't answer me and I twisted away from his shoulder, looking at him, momentarily disturbed. His eyes did not see me. They were looking at something I could not see and in that brief, unguarded moment, were filled with inexpressible grief. Then, conscious of my stare he smiled, his expression changing, pulling me closer to him.

"I'm happier, Jenny Wren. Definitely happier." And his hand slid round my body, pulling me closely to him, so that I could feel his heart beating beneath the thinness of his shirt, smell not only his after-shave, but the sweat brought on by our clamber down the bank, smell the maleness of him, so that when he bent his head to mine and kissed me it was no ordinary flirtatious kiss, but a letting loose of suppressed misery. An acknowledgement that in each other we had found the solace we had been seeking. My arms tightened around his neck, my fingers burrowing in his hair, my tongue flickering in answer to his, passion that I never knew existed, rising in me like a tide. Eternities later we parted. For a fleeting second disbelief chased the desire from his eyes to be replaced by what I had been praying to see there.

"Jenny Wren," he said, his finger-tip tracing the curve of my cheek, resting gently under my chin, tilting it upwards. "Jenny Wren, you certainly are something."

"The feeling," I said shakily, "is mutual."

Gently he raised me to my feet, and with his arm around my shoulder and mine around his waist, we made our way slowly, and both slightly stunned at the suddenness with which love had overtaken us, to the car.

Five

That evening when I entered the dining-room, Manuel hurried over to me, a knowledgeable smile on his friendly face. Gently he directed me not to my own table, but to Jonathan's. As Manuel left with our orders I said:–

"You realize you've wrecked my reputation!"

"In the eyes of the waiters your reputation was wrecked the minute you stepped into my car. And don't think they don't know. I could practically see the receptionist dashing off with the news as we left! Sitting at separate tables would fool nobody!"

"Then I'm glad my reputation has gone to the winds. Eating together is far nicer than eating alone."

"It certainly is." His hand closed firmly over mine, sending my flesh tingling.

After we had returned to the hotel from our trip to Valenca I had spent a thoughtful hour in the bath. Although there had been many men who had said they were in love with me, and with whom I had even felt slightly in love in return, I had never before experienced the bodily reactions I had that afternoon when Jonathan had kissed me so passionately. He hadn't repeated it. As we parted to go to our own rooms to change for dinner his kiss had been warm and stirring, but the blaze of passion he had shown earlier had either died or been held in check. By the look in his eyes I knew that it hadn't died. What had happened had been as much of a surprise to him as it had to me. Love had been the last thing Jonathan had expected to find on his travels through Spain and Portugal. He was like a tiger on a lead. Again I felt the stirring of excitement deep within me. How long would it be before the tiger broke the self imposed lead and passion flared so nakedly again? And what would I do when it did? So far I had remained a virgin. Something Rozalinda found highly amusing. But previously the temptation had never been strong enough for me to put behind me the strict moral teaching with which Aunt Harriet had brought me up. It was now. Slowly I towelled myself dry. One thing at least was clear. I would never marry Phil.

"It's market day tomorrow at Barcelos. Do you fancy going?" Jonathan was asking.

"Oh yes, I'd love to." If he'd asked if I wanted to go to the moon I would have agreed.

"And just where have your thoughts been for the last ten minutes? I've already asked if you'd like to go to Oporto, Braga, or Ponte de Barca and all without an answer."

"Someday," I said blushing, "I might just tell you!"

After dinner we strolled hand in hand onto the terrace, making our way leisurely down the moss covered steps that led into the mimosa scented trees. One huge oak soared above the rest, and beneath it was a wooden bench. We sat down, leaning against the trunk of the tree. Below us the leaves and branches soughed in the gentle night breeze and from far below us came the distant roar of the Atlantic swell, the crest of the waves ghostly white in the darkness.

Tenderly he pulled me closer, raising my face to his, his lips seeking mine. Again there was warmth and desire in his kiss. But there was also restraint. I wondered why. There seemed to be only one explanation. I asked, scarcely breathing:—

"Jonathan. Are you married?"

I felt his body stiffen against mine, and then he said:—

"No. Not now."

The inflection in his voice was enough to prevent me from probing further. Whoever his wife had been she had certainly left deep scars. Scars that were not yet fully healed. But then, I thought to myself, nestling into his shoulder, I was a nurse. A good nurse could achieve amazing results in a week. Especially if her heart was in it.

At the Barcelos market the next day Jonathan bought me a garish, over-sized pottery cockerel that was the local emblem. We both agreed that painted black with scarlet plumage and vividly painted hearts and flowers all over it, it was the epitome of bad taste but unbelievably splendid. I knew that it was going to grace my dressing-table for years to come, mystifying my friends and relations. Let them wonder. I didn't care. Whenever I saw it I would remember Jonathan, for that reason alone it was priceless.

In the next few days, fortified by innumerable bags of sugared almonds, lots of cream filled pastries and the delicious local wine, we visited Braga, peeping into the dark and forbidding cathedral and quickly out again, the National Park, an area of mountains and lakes, vying with rushing rivers and vast forests of pine. The guidebook said that the area abounded in deer, wolves, martens, badgers and wild boar. I could well believe it. The upper flanks of the mountains were so vast and desolate that it wouldn't have surprised me to find even bears. We *did* see some wolves. But they were safely behind a high barrier of wire netting in a large tree filled compound. They looked just as mean and nasty as I expected them to. In a far flung pousada, we ate tiny pieces of unnamed fish deliciously fried in batter and served with rice and fresh lettuce, squeezing great wedges of lemon over the whole. The bread was butterless but still warm from the oven, the wine unnamed and cheaper than mineral water. It also had a pretty devastating effect and we spent the rest of the afternoon laying on a river bank, bare feet dangling into icy water, alternately talking and laughing and kissing. Another day we set out for Chaves. A small town scores of miles from even the nearest village, by the time we reached it, passing through country that changed dramatically from mountainous to endless stretches of peat and heather reminiscent of Scotland, it was already tea-time. Exhausted, and dreading the thought of the night drive back on a road fit only for four legged animals, we hastily found a cafe and revived ourselves with coffee. Not the coffee of the hotel but strong, dark liquid that came in thimble size cups. Then came the moment that made the whole long journey worthwhile. As we began to see what Chaves had to offer, and on first sight it seemed to have very little, we looked into the first of a street of shops. The whole window was taken up with only one article. A huge dinner service priced at a thousand escudos and depicting scenes of Stratford-On-Avon, Ann Hathaway's Cottage and the Globe Theatre, the names all written in English! It was too much.

"You mean I've fought my way all those miles into this barren hinterland, ruining my car, and all for the sake of the chance to buy a Willie Shakespeare dinner set I would get any day in Woolwich market!" Jonathan said indignantly.

Oblivious of the curious stares of the local inhabitants, we laughed our way up the dusty street, looking in vain for any sight that might justify our journey. There wasn't one, so we returned to the Lamborgini, Jonathan gritting his teeth manfully as his precious car bounced once more onto the pot-holed road. I slept most of the way back. A deep, dreamless sleep, that left me feeling I had regained the mental peace which I had been seeking so long.

The days slipped by. Friday, the day Jonathan was leaving to visit his friend in Vigo rapidly approached and still nothing was said between us of the future. The Thursday night as I brushed my hair and sprayed on my perfume, my heart felt tight within my chest. Although the moment at Valenca had never been repeated, it *had* happened. I had seen the expression in his eyes. I *knew* it was more than a holiday romance. What could Jonathan's wife possibly have done that had left such an obviously strong and self sufficient man too frightened to love again. I paused as I put in a pearl earring. Perhaps the answer was that he still loved her. It was a chilling thought.

For me, dinner was strained, though Jonathan talked happily about our afternoon visit to Caminho and the woman we had seen, dressed entirely in white and with a cockerel on her head. Jonathan had thought she was some sort of fortune-teller, but on enquiring from the locals, was told that she was simply mad. I was barely listening. I was wondering how to bring up the subject of the morning when he would drive away leaving me behind. Dreading to hear any cliched words of what fun it had been, how glad he had been to meet me ...

"Let's go for a walk on the beach," he said as Manuel cleared the last of our plates away. Holding his hand tightly, I followed him out of the room and through reception to the car park. Neither of us spoke as the

Lamborgini roared its powerful way down the swooping bends and into the town. Minutes later the busy streets were behind us and we were on a small road that backed the dunes, the air warm, heavy with the tang of sea-spray and the sweetness of pines.

I still wore my evening dress and sandals and I slipped my sandals off, enjoying the feeling of the sand as it slipped between my toes. It was a pale sickle of silver, the sea a glittering mass, broken by the giant white horses that reared their heads, crashing down onto the beach in swirling eddies of foam.

Hand in hand we walked along the untrodden sand.

I said at last:– "It's Friday tomorrow."

"Yes, and you go to your friends at Ofir."

"And you go to your friends in Vigo."

We stopped, gazing into each other's eyes and I knew that in mine the agony of the parting was blatantly apparent.

He led me across the dunes, sitting down in their shelter, resting against them. I curled up beside him, waiting as I had never waited before. I thought he was going to speak, but instead he groaned, a sound that came from deep within him, savagely slamming his fist into the sand and then I was in his arms, and this time there was no holding back in his kisses, the passion I knew was there was finally unleashed as his hands knotted themselves in my hair, making me cry out in a mixture of pain and pleasure, and his mouth came down on mine, hard and demanding. Everything that was in me responded, I wanted my body closer to his. Closer and closer. His tongue searched my mouth, his hands moving from my hair to my body, pushing aside the chiffon folds of my bodice, cradling my breasts. Then his hand was on my naked leg, its heat searing through me as it travelled upwards and he said chokingly; "Jenny, Jenny, Jenny ..."

Hungrily I pulled the weight of him down on top of me and then, so suddenly that I felt I'd been stabbed, he jumped to his feet, standing over me, struggling for breath ... and control. It can only have been a brief second but it seemed like an eternity. Then, his passion in check, he sat down again, drawing me close.

Of all the crazy unexpected things I expected him to say, what he did say took my breath away.

"Let's get married, Jenny Wren."

"Oh God," I could barely speak for relief and surprise and wonder. "Oh God, yes please."

Slowly he let out his breath and I said:– "But if you want to marry me, why ... this. Why did you stop?"

"Because, Jenny Wren," he said, his voice full of love and undisguised amusement. "Because I'm a man of twenty-nine who has not only been previously married for several years but has sown more than his share of wild oats, and I can tell a virgin at fifteen paces."

"For goodness sake ...," I began to laugh and cry at the same time, "has that been your reason for behaving so differently after Valenca?"

"That and a few other things. I didn't think I would ever feel that mixture of passion and tenderness for another woman as long as I lived. It took me some time to get used to the idea."

"I'm glad you did."

He grinned. "What do you say about meeting me in a weeks time at Ofir?"

"Oh that would be super! You could meet my Aunt and friends ..."

He said gently, "What's the matter, Jenny?"

I stared unspeaking at the white breakers as they crashed

relentlessly on the beach. If I didn't tell him, Rozalinda would. If not Rozalinda, then someone else. Besides I wanted no secrets from Jonathan. Now was the time to tell him.

"You don't know everything about me, Jonathan. There's things in my past that might make you change your mind about marrying me."

"Jenny Wren, there is nothing, nothing that could make me change my mind about that."

"Then I'd like to tell you now."

"No. Not now. I can see that it's going to distress you. I don't intend having the memories of tonight spoilt. There'll be enough time at Ofir for us to tell each other whatever we need to about our past lives." He took me in his arms, silencing my weak protests with kisses that drove every other thought away.

Six

He left after breakfast the next morning. An hour or two later I finished my packing, paid my bill, and eased the Volkswagen onto the now familiar road into Viana. I drove south with a light heart, waving cheerily to the children as they helped in the fields or led enormous looking cows to graze, rocking through the dusty villages, painfully aware that the Volkswagen's springs did not match up to those of the Lamborgini.

It was just after midday when I reached the road sign for Ofir. I turned right, narrowly avoiding a peasant woman sat on a stool in the middle of the road, hopefully holding up a repellant looking eel. On one side of me a river ran broadly towards the sea, on the other were the beginnings of the lush pinewoods Aunt Harriet so enjoyed. Very soon the woods were on either side, enticing pathways leading into their depths. I emerged to overlook sand dunes ... and the large four star hotel that Harold had tried so unsuccessfully to buy. A sandy track barely wide enough to take the car, led away from the hotel, bumping unevenly into the woods. After a few hundred yards I caught a glimpse of white stucco and a roof of gleaming beechwood.

It was sufficiently unlike anything else I had seen in Portugal to convince me that I had at last reached Rozalinda's 'Enclave'. Slowly I bumped nearer and then stopped. There was no-one about. The woods were silent except for the sound of the birds that flashed between the branches in a dazzle of colour.

The villa was set high overlooking the sea, the gardens at the rear, that ran down to the track and the woods, a feast of flowers and miniature fountains, with a small stream falling from pool to pool, its banks thick with yellow and pink lilies. Large picture windows gave a glimpse of white painted walls, and what looked at a distance to be a gigantic Picasso. Stone steps curved down, leading through the garden into the villa close by. This was much smaller but far prettier. Here the walls were covered in the Portuguese way, with richly coloured tiles, wooden shutters were thrown back to reveal window ledges crammed with begonias and trailing lobelia. The upper storey was surrounded by a narrow wooden balcony, and beside a wicker chair and table I could see a sun-hat that belonged to Aunt Harriet and her knitting bag, balls of wool cascading over the wooden slats. I stepped out of the car and instead of going straight to what was presumably Rozalinda's villa, walked around and passed the smaller one. A cluster of trees shielded it from the rest of the enclave, but the stone steps swirled round in a picturesque arc from Aunt Harriet's front door fading into a path between the trees and then leading up in a fresh meandering series of steps to two pink washed villas with wrought iron balconies and scarlet tiled roofs. I climbed the steps and turned seawards, catching my breath as I did so.

An endless stretch of silver sand curved away in either direction. Huge breakers reared to an awe-inspiring height far out in the distance crashing down in a white foaming mass, to rear rhythmically once more, till at last they reached the shore in a frothing swirl of spray. Controlling the temptation to run barefoot down to the sea, I turned, the long grass of the dunes brushing against my legs as I contemplated the two villas. One of them must be Mary and Tom's, and one Phil's. Perhaps I was to share with Aunt Harriet. I opened the tiny gate that led into the surrounding gardens and peeped through the windows. A large through fireplace separated a dining-room and a salon, and on the plain walls hung a large beautifully carved cherub. I couldn't imagine Phil living with it, and mentally categorised the villa as Mary's. In no hurry I followed the moss covered path to the adjoining villa. Here the walls were covered in gleaming pine, a large marble topped table dwarfing one room surrounded by pink velvet covered chairs, the living area scattered with brilliantly coloured rugs and luxurious looking settees. A few magazines scattered on a side table and an empty cup and saucer were the only signs of habitation. There was no sign of a piano. I strolled round to the rear, dropping down onto the pathway and the pines, looking around me. As I did so I caught the first notes of Liszt's piano concerto Number One drifting through the trees. I smiled and began to walk deeper into the pines towards the source of the music.

The other three villas were out of sight of the rest of the enclave. They were grouped fairylike in a dell in the woods, and from the nearest one came the familiar beautiful notes and I could see the back of Phil's head, bent in total preoccupation as he played. I didn't interrupt him but sat down leaning my back against one of the trees, caught up in the magic of Phil's playing. It was the perfect accompaniment to the new found joy that was in my heart.

Too soon, he finished, and as he mopped his brow and lifted his hands to begin another piece, I stood up calling out:– "Phil!"

He turned immediately, his usually serious expression breaking into a wide smile.

"Jennifer! I thought you were never coming."

We met simultaneously in the doorway and he caught me in a hug.

"Another two days and I was coming to Viana for you. I would have done earlier but Aunt Harriet said to give you a full week on your own."

Silently I blessed Aunt Harriet. Phil's arrival a few days earlier would only have complicated matters.

"I've been sight-seeing … and making friends."

He held me away from him, looking closely at my face.

"Thank God for that. I thought you'd gone into a deep depression."

"No. That's all behind me, Phil. Truly it is."

He led the way into a large room filled with two grand pianos and several giant cushions scattered on the floor.

"It will take too long to make coffee. Fancy a Coke?" he asked, walking into a small kitchen. "I want to know who this friend of yours is that kept you away so long. You could easily have sight-seen from here you know. We're not far from the National Park." He came back with two ice-cold glasses clinking with ice. "I'll take you tomorrow."

"I've already been," I said, taking the glass from his hand, then, seeing the flash of disappointment in his eyes, said hurriedly. "But you could spend a month there and still not see half of it. If you haven't been yet I shall be able to act as guide."

"Presumably she was English," Phil said, lounging

comfortably on the floor cushions. "Was she holidaying by herself?"

I sank down beside him, cradling the drink in my hands.

"It wasn't a she, Phil. It was a he."

He stiffened, and I hated myself for the hurt I knew I was going to cause him. I said, taking hold of his hand.

"His name is Jonathan and he *was* holidaying alone." It seemed useless to beat about the bush. I said simply. "And I love him."

Phil's glass remained perfectly steady. There was a moment's silence and then he said:–

"You were only in Viana a week, Jennifer."

"I know. But it happened."

Slowly he put his glass down, looking at me steadily. "I don't think you're well enough to make those kind of statements yet."

"But I am Phil. I'm perfectly well."

"You weren't when I last saw you and that was only a few weeks ago, do you think at the moment that you're the best judge?"

"Yes I do. You're quite right when you say I wasn't fully recovered a few weeks ago. I was still depressed and having nightmares and feeling life would never be the same again. Meeting Jonathan has changed all that for me. *Please* be happy for me Phil. When you meet him, you'll understand."

He raised his eyebrows. "You mean you've brought him with you?"

"No. He's visiting friends in Vigo. He's coming down next weekend."

"For the official seal of approval," Phil said, and I could tell by the tone of his voice that the worst was over.

"Something like that. You'll like him, Phil, I know you will."

"Any friend of yours is a friend of mine," he said wryly. "Tell me about him. Where does he come from?"

I shrugged my shoulders. "I've no idea," and then laughed at the expression on Phil's face.

"No, really Phil. I'm telling the truth. He's English, twenty-nine, has blond hair and his eyes ..." I paused, feeling my spine tingle as I remembered the effect Jonathan's eyes had on me when he looked at me with desire. "His eyes are hazel and he's about five foot ten and has nice hands and ..."

"For goodness sake," Phil said with fond exasperation. "You'll be telling me what shape his feet are next! I'm not interested in whether he's blond, black or covered in navy-blue dots. What is he? Butcher, baker, or candlestick-maker?"

"I haven't a clue. He could be a stock-broker or a postman. All I know is that I love him."

"For two people who have spent a week in each other's company you've made up your mind dangerously fast without knowing much about him."

"I know enough to have said I'll marry him."

Phil's eyes widened, and it was a few seconds before he spoke. When he did he let his breath out through his teeth. "Well, I suppose a proposal of marriage is proof his intentions are honourable."

I thought of the beach at Viana. "His intentions," I said, "are strictly honourable. Where is everyone? All the other villas are deserted."

"They've all gone to visit friends of Miles in Oporto."

"Miles? Miles who?"

"Rozalinda's last leading man. You've met him before.

He was at my party ..." he broke off, his face flushing.

I squeezed his hand. "I'm over it, Phil. I wasn't joking. I remember him vaguely. Good-looking in a flashy sort of way. Somewhere in his mid-thirties."

"That's him," Phil said, relief in his voice. "He's down here trying to persuade Rozalinda to take up a film part she's been offered."

"What's the matter? Is it too small for her?"

"No. According to Miles it's tailor-made for her. It's a million dollar film with Rozalinda as the Queen of Sheba. Only Rozalinda isn't interested."

"What bait has been more attractive?"

"That's just it. Nothing. She says she's in need of a rest."

I stared unbelievingly. "You mean Rozalinda's turned down this part to stay on here with *Harold*?"

Phil nodded.

I shook my head in disbelief.

"Actually, she *does* look a bit off it. Very nervy these days. Old Harold's being very protective towards her."

"He always is and she usually can't wait to get away."

"Not this time. Anyway, you'll be able to see for yourself in a few hours time. They're coming back for dinner. We all eat en masse over at Rozalinda's." He grimaced at the prospect and I laughed.

"Poor Phil. Is she beginning to get you down."

"She *always* gets me down. I can't imagine why she invited me in the first place."

I could have told him but didn't. Instead I said:—

"And how is Mary?"

"Seems all right. I think she's missing the children but Tom is having a great time. The lap of luxury suits him."

"And Aunt Harriet?"

"Oh, she's fine," Phil sounded vague which didn't

surprise me. He generally had to be hit on the head before he noticed anything. The fact that he was aware of Rozalinda's nervous state was probably only due to Miles spelling it out for him, and I couldn't believe he'd got it right. Rozalinda being temperamental, yes. Suffering from nerves to the extent of turning down a major film role, no.

"Play some more Liszt," I said, settling myself comfortably back against the cushions. "It was heaven listening to you play. I hadn't realised how long it's been."

Phil knew how long it had been. It had been the night of his party when he had played 'Claire de Lune', at Aunt Harriet's request. After that there had been no opportunity to listen to Phil play again. Only various cells and then the psychiatric clinic.

Understandingly he put his glass down and seated himself at the piano. This time he played the Hungarian Rhapsody and before the last beautiful strains had died away I was sound asleep.

When I awoke I could hear the distant slamming of car doors and Phil was saying unenthusiastically:—

"They're back. I suppose we'd better go and let them know you've arrived." His face brightened. "*And* give them your news. *That* will give Rozalinda something to think about!"

Arm in arm we walked over the soft pine needles towards Rozalinda's villa. I could hear Aunt Harriet saying briskly:—

"Her car is here so she must be down at Phil's ..." and Mary saying:— "If I'd known she was coming this afternoon I would never have gone out. How awful for there to be no-one to have welcomed her."

"Phil isn't no-one darling," Rozalinda was saying in her affected drawl, and then we were in the doorway and

Rozalinda's arms were spread wide in an extravagant gesture as she said:–

"Darling ..." kissing me on the cheek, and I was once again surrounded, quite literally, by family and friends.

Seven

With difficulty I extricated myself from Rozalinda's extravagant embrace. She seemed to think the more demonstrative her affection the more she was helping me over the crisis in my life. Her sense of drama would be quite affronted to find that I was no longer suffering but joyously happy. Aunt Harried kissed me and as my arms folded round her I realised with shock that she was losing weight, her small body almost bird-like in my arms. I looked at her with concern. Her eyes were alight with welcome, but there were signs of strain on her face that Phil had been too blind to see. I mentally decided that at the first suitable moment I would have a private chat with Aunt Harriet about her health. It wouldn't be easy. She regarded herself as immune to any sort of bodily weakness and when my father had been alive had driven him to distraction by stubbornly refusing to take any notice of him.

Mary hugged me tightly. "Jenny, we were so worried. Why on earth didn't you come straight here?" then, without waiting for an answer. "Phil wanted to go to Viana and fetch you, but Aunt Harriet said she had spoken to you and that you sounded fine ..." her expression of anxiety changed to one of surprise as she let go of me and saw my face clearly for the first time. "You *look* fine! Dearest Jenny, you look really *well!*"

"I am, Mary. I am." I said, as Tom grasped my hand. "There's been no need for you to worry at all."

"Yes, but ..." Mary began protestingly.

Our eyes met and a silent message passed. It meant what it had meant since we were children and wanted to talk about something in private, see you later. Her anxiety faded, but like Aunt Harriet I thought I could detect lines of worry that had not been there when I had last seen her in Templar's Way. The thought that the strain on the two faces of people I loved had been caused solely by my week in Viana came with an onrush of guilt. I squashed it almost immediately. I had finished with feelings of guilt. If I had wanted to take a week's holiday by myself I was perfectly entitled to do so, and as I had spoken to Aunt Harriet, reassuring her as to my health, there had been no reason for anyone to have worried to the extent that even my arrival didn't dispell the anxiety. It was something else that was disturbing Aunt Harriet and Mary. I would know what it was in due course.

"Darling, you remember Miles Sullivan, don't you?" Rozalinda was saying, leading me by a perfectly manicured hand to a darkly handsome face.

Miles smiled. "Nice to meet you again, Jenny. I hear you've been staying at the Santa Luzia. Nice hotel. I stayed there myself a couple of years ago. Very Rivieraish if I remember."

"Yes. It's very quiet at the moment. There's only a handful of people there. The rush starts this next couple of weeks."

"Then you were wise to leave," he said, his smile

intimate as if we shared a secret.

I smiled and turned back to Mary. Rozalinda flung her arms wide, spinning round in a circle and collapsing onto a plushly upholstered chair.

"Isn't this just *too, too* much. Darling Jenny with us and our party complete! I think it calls for a celebration. Champagne, Harold, tell Maria we want iced champagne."

I had only had the briefest glimpse of Harold, hovering with beaming smile on the edge of the circle, Rozalinda's back firmly seeing to it that he kept off the centre of her stage.

Her expression changed to one of deep sorrow, the sympathy of one who fully understands another's suffering.

"Jenny. Jenny *Darling*. You shouldn't have stayed in that silly old hotel moping by yourself when we were all here waiting for you and knowing only too well what you were going through. No ..." she raised a hand dramatically to prevent my protests. "We *do* know, and that's why we wanted you here. To forget, amongst those who love you most."

"She's not likely to forget anything with you reminding her all the time," Phil said bluntly.

She looked sorrowfully at him. "You're a man. You couldn't possibly understand. But *we* do. Don't we, Mary?"

Mary smiled and tried not to look embarrassed ... I laughed.

"You're wasting your sympathy, Rozalinda. I'm going to enjoy holidaying with you all here, but I'm not in *need* of it. I'm not an invalid you know."

Rozalinda pouted prettily. "Not *bodily*, darling, but ..."

"Oh, cut it out Roz," Phil said bad-temperedly. She glared at him. Being called Roz wasn't part of Rozalinda's image.

"Yes," Harold said unexpectedly, "No more references to the past, what?"

Before his wife could shoot him down in pieces, Aunt Harriet rallied to the rescue.

"Very sensible, Harold. That champagne looks frozen not chilled. I'm sure it would help if one of us could speak enough Portuguese to tell Maria what we want properly. Poor child, it's not her fault ..."

"It is," Rozalinda said, rising from her languorous position as it was no longer claiming attention. "Good God, the girl should at least speak English. I thought *everyone* could speak English!"

A smile hovered on Phil's lips. He knew she was perfectly serious.

"I think she does very well," Harold said with the air of one who knew he was being brave and was justly proud of the fact. "At least the other maids do everything she tells them."

"Where *are* the vast army of servants?" I asked. Rozalinda never travelled without a private secretary, her own hairdresser, her personal maid, as well as cook and butler and several dogs-bodies.

"They come every morning," Aunt Harriet said. "There's not enough room for them to live in. Only Maria stays through the day. She cooks and serves the evening meal and then goes home."

"Where to? There doesn't seem to be a village for miles."

"There's one the other side of the estuary. I think she comes from there," Rozalinda said airily. It was typical of her that she didn't know.

"I've seen to it that a taxi comes to collect her and also brings her and the other girls every morning," Harold said. I smiled at him. He might not be the best company in the world, but at least he was human. Seeing that the girl got home safely in the dark would never have occurred to his wife.

"And what about your hairdresser, etc., etc., etc.?" I asked.

Rozalinda shrugged. "I wanted a complete rest, darling. Only those who are *truly* close to me."

For a dreadful minute I thought Phil was going to put his foot in it, but then Tom was saying:–

"And that's what you've got. An intimate house-party with no outsiders. Who could ask for anything more?"

The champagne popped and frothed, our glasses were filled, and Rozalinda was radiant once more as Tom toasted her as hostess, her arm protectively around my shoulders, her heavy perfume filling the air.

A young girl stood hesitantly on the threshold and Harold turned to her. "Ready are we, Maria? Good. Come on. Into the dining-room."

Rozalinda sat at the head of the table. Harold at the foot. On either side of Rozalinda sat Tom and Phil, then Mary and I were seated opposite each other, and then Miles next to me and opposite Aunt Harriet. There wasn't going to be much opportunity for private conversation with either Aunt Harriet or Mary, and the more I saw of them, the more worried I was becoming. The signs of strains, partly hidden by relief at my arrival, were now only too transparent. Rozalinda's seating arrangements gave Mary no chance for any words of privacy with Tom, and throughout the meal she kept trying to catch his eye, but she was no match for Rozalinda who kept up a constant flirtatious chatter with both him and Phil. As she was their hostess, neither man could do much but respond. Though Phil's eyes kept glancing in my direction, a smile of secret amusement on his mouth. I knew very well that any minute he was going to steal Rozalinda's thunder and at my expense. I would have preferred to tell Aunt Harriet first about Jonathan and privately, but could see the temptation was going to be too much for Phil.

As Rozalinda finally paused for breath and daintily speared a mushroom with her fork, Phil said:—

"I believe Jennifer has a friend she would like to ask down for a few days."

Only Phil ever referred to me as Jennifer. His smile as he turned towards me was filled with so much complicity that my exasperation changed to one of shared amusement.

"Darling, but of course! Is it someone you met at Viana?"

I nodded.

"How lovely. Of *course* she can stay. There's plenty of room in your villa for two people. I'll get one of the maids to make up the extra bed tomorrow."

I tried to avoid Phil's eyes.

"I'm afraid it isn't so simple, Rozalinda."

"Why of course it is." She leant impulsively forward, brushing between Tom and his dinner, clasping my hand. "If she's a friend and you would like her to stay then of course she can stay. I know ...," she went on as I opened my mouth to explain. "I know Tom's just said how lovely it was to be together with no outsiders, but you can't *possibly* think I would object to a girl friend of yours staying for a few days."

"It isn't a girl friend," I said as Rozalinda released me, allowing Tom to see his plate once more instead of Rozalinda's over exposed breasts. "It's a man."

For once the centre of attention was taken well and truly away from Rozalinda.

Phil said with blatant pleasure:– "So you see Roz. Making up the other bed in Jennifer's villa could be a little compromising. I don't think Jennifer is quite into the film scene set of morals yet."

Rozalinda ignored any insult Phil's remarks disguised.

"Darling, how wonderful! So *that's* why you've been hiding away from us. You must tell us all about him. Who is he and where did you meet ..."

"His name is Jonathan Brown and I met him at the Santa Luzia."

"Don't ask for any more details. She doesn't know them." Phil said wickedly.

Aunt Harriet cut across Rozalinda's stream of questions, "When is he coming, Jenny?"

"At the end of the week. He's visiting friends in Vigo at the moment."

"A holiday romance!" Rozalinda was rhapsodising. "What a wonderful start to your stay in Portugal!"

"It's not a holiday romance," I said, this time not looking at her but at Aunt Harriet. "I'm going to marry him."

I saw the same thoughts chase through Aunt Harriet's mind as had gone through Phil's. My eyes smiled at her, willing her to understand that I wasn't acting unreasonably or in reaction to what had happened in the past months. Something of my new found confidence must have transmitted itself, because I saw her shoulders, which had stiffened at the news, relax.

"*Marry* him!" Mary said happily. "Oh Jenny, I *am* pleased."

"Me too," Tom said, turning and shaking my hand. "Congratulations Jenny."

"Alow me to offer you my congratulations as well," Miles said, holding my hand for longer than necessary. "I think this calls for more champagne, don't you Rozalinda?''

For a fleeting second there was an expressiosn on her face that made her look suddenly old, somfhing that wasn't meant to be seen. Then she was her usual self, clapping her hands high above her head, her gold bracelets tinkling down sun-tanned arms, demanding that Harold uncork more champagne and saying she just couldn't *wait* to see Jenny's Jonathan.

For the next few minutes I was able to sit back and watch them all. That brief glimpse of Rozalinda had reminded me of what Phil had said. That she was virtually hiding at Ofir, and that not even Miles' visit had managed to lure her away and into a major film part.

It was hard to tell if she was genuinely in need of a rest or not. Rozalinda's play acting never ceased and I had long ago given up the attempt to discover what her real feelings were about anything or anyone. Her blue-black hair hung in a cloud around her face, her eyes a brilliant, compelling violet. That she had been born with grey ones hadn't deterred Rozalinda. Violet eyes were more photogenic. Soft contact lenses saw to it that she had them. The same was true of her hair. As a child it had been mouse-brown, I didn't fancy anyone's chances of surviving if they reminded her of the fact now. Aunt Harriet had once told me in amused exasperation, that Rozalinda had destroyed all her childhood photographs in case any enterprising pressman should get hold of one of them. Rozalinda was a *natural* beauty. And that meant that her violet eyes and blue-black hair were natural too! Phil had said callously that she had also had her breasts operated on. Certainly they were breathtaking and I couldn't remember them being quite so awe-inspiring when we were in Templar's Way, but how

Phil, of all people, would know a detail like that was beyond me. Rozalinda was Rozalinda. Bright. Sparkling. Flirtatious. Demanding constant attention. But tonight there was something else as well. A brittleness under the gay laughter that I had never noticed before. Perhaps she *was* under pressure. Being a constant sex symbol couldn't be easy.

Phil, satisfied with his mischief making, was looking more like a little boy than ever. His auburn hair curled attractively around a regular featured face that was usually too serious. Aunt Harriet said it was only my company that brought out the light-hearted side of him. What he needed was someone who would love him and with whom he would feel as much in tune as he did with me. And who, hopefully, he loved in return. I sometimes doubted Phil's ability to love physically. He had once had a brief affair with an older woman. She expected nothing more from him than he was prepared to give, yet he had broken off the relationship suddenly, saying that he had found out it wasn't her first affair and that it made him feel unclean. It seemed to me an unnatural attitude to take. She wasn't promiscuous and surely he couldn't have expected a woman of twenty-nine to have remained a virgin. But Phil had. The fact that he had no serious intentions towards her didn't signify. If there had been any other affairs I knew nothing of them. As far as I knew, and I was sure I knew pretty well, Phil's life was celibate.

The way Rozalinda was teasing and flirting with him, I wondered if I wouldn't be doing her a favour by telling her what I knew. She might have seduced every other man she had wanted, but she would never get Phil into bed with her in a million years. Purity of the soul was what Phil was looking for. Despite her many other attributes, purity was definitely

not on Rozalinda's list. Failing to get the answering banter
from Phil, Rozalinda was turning her attention more and
more to Tom. I felt sorry for Mary having to watch Tom
manfully respond to his hostess's flirtation. Though
perhaps Tom wasn't finding it so hard. Rozalinda was
undeniably beautiful and when she wanted to turn on the
charm she could do it at a full blast. It was a charm that
worked only on the opposite sex, but it certainly worked,
and seeing the hurt in Mary's eyes I began to feel annoyed.
I accepted a helping of the delicious looking sweet,
determined to have a private word with Rozalinda
afterwards. It was unfair of her to ruin Mary's holiday by
teasing Tom for want of another more suitable admirer.
She lifted her eyes at that exact moment, narrowing them
on Miles' unseeing head. I had a glimmer of the answer in
that look. Suddenly sure that Rozalinda was only flirting
with Tom to make Miles jealous. I remembered back to the
night of Phil's party and the gossip that had been current at
the time. That Miles and Rozalinda were having an affair.
If the affair had lasted and she was wanting to provoke him,
then the only other males she was able to do it with were
Tom and Phil, and as Phil wasn't playing it had to be Tom.
I wondered if Harold was even slightly aware. He didn't
look it. He sat at the foot of the table, corpulent as ever,
beaming at all and sundry, seemingly oblivious of his wife's
neglect.

Miles said softly to me:– "Rozalinda is in fine form, don't
you think?"

"If you're meaning what I think you mean. Yes." I said
shortly.

He laughed. "I'm glad you've come. I don't like to see
innocent little creatures getting hurt."

I said equally softly, my voice tinged with anger, "Are you referring to Mary?"

"Who else?" he said in mock surprise. "Rozalinda doesn't mean it of course. She flirts with everyone. It's a reflex action, but I don't think little brown mouse understands that."

"Mary is *not* a little brown mouse!" I said, and then as Aunt Harriet looked enquiringly across the table, lowered my voice even further. "If you've got anything else to say I think it would be wisest to leave it till later."

"With pleasure," he said, giving me the benefit of a gleaming smile and teasing eyes. Rozalinda wasn't the only compulsive flirt who sat at the dinner table.

Deliberately I turned to Rozalinda, interrupting her as she playfully pinched Tom's cheek.

"I still don't know which villa is mine, Rozalinda. Is it one of those near to Phil's?"

"Yes. Mary and Tom and Aunt Harriet have the two villas nearest this one. Phil and Miles have one each in the woods and the third is all ready for you. When Jonathan comes we'll have to put him up with Phil or Miles."

"He's more than welcome to share with me. There's not enough room in Phil's," Miles said generously. "Besides, I won't be here for much longer."

His eyes and Rozalinda's held.

"Just till our business affairs are tied up."

"Not now, not now," Harold said hastily. "Don't spoil a nice evening by talking business."

Phil's eyebrows raised slightly as he looked across at me, signalling 'I told you so'. Certainly the mention of business affairs had taken the smile from Rozalinda's mouth and replaced it with a look of sulky defiance.

Miles turned to me, saying pleasantly:– "Rozalinda is to star as the Queen of Sheba in a mammoth spectacular. Perfect casting, don't you think?"

Rozalinda's chair scraped back sharply and she rose to her feet her eyes flaming. Harold said nervously:–

"Later old man, later. Rozalinda is tired at the moment. No time to be talking business." His eyes full of concern he hurried the length of the table and took her arm. She jerked it away, turning and sweeping into the salon.

There was a short embarrassed silence and then Tom excused himself from the table and hurried after her, followed equally quickly by Aunt Harriet.

"You seem to have successfully wrecked the dinner," I said to Miles.

"That, you will find, is easy done," he said lightly, rising to his feet and taking his glass of wine with him. For the first time in her life, Mary avoided my eyes leaving the table and her scarcely touched wine.

"I thought," I said to Phil, my voice heavy with sarcasm, "that you said everything was fine here except that Rozalinda was a little nervy."

"I did."

"Then you must be blind."

He looked genuinely surprised. "You mean Rozalinda storming out like that? That's an everyday occurrence, always has been."

"I mean," I said, wondering just how unseeing Phil could possibly be. "Rozalinda flirting mercilessly with Tom and making Mary intensely unhappy. I mean Aunt Harriet being obviously unwell. I mean the fact that there's more to the Miles-Rozalinda relationship than co-stars, and that there's an atmosphere under all this gaiety that you could cut with a knife."

"That's just what Mary said as she left the table," Phil said, helping himself to more fruit flan.

"What, that you could cut the air with a knife?"

"No." said Phil innocently, "that she wished she had one."

Eight

Rozalinda had regained her composure by the time Phil and myself joined the rest of the party in the next room. She swept across taking me by the arm.

"I *must* apologise for Miles, darling. It was too, *too* bad of him to provoke me like that on your first evening here. He knows I don't want this beastly film part and I shall be glad when he goes. He's making me quite ill."

"It sounds a good part, there's not that many million dollar films to turn down these days."

Her mouth took on an obstinate line. "I'm not doing it. I'm staying here ... with Harold. Why, we hardly see anything of each other!"

Seeing Harold had never been one of her priorities in life.

The laugh was back as Tom approached us. "I'm just apologising to Jenny for Miles bullying," she said, pouting.

Tom was instant sympathy. "Just because he's frightened of being replaced in the film if you turn your part down. If you want him to leave, tell him so. Can't he see he's making you ill with his pestering? If you want me to have a word with him ..."

She laid a hand delicately on his arm, lashes fluttering.

"Darling Tom. Always so considerate. How lucky Mary is. No, Miles was my co-star in my last film, and," she drew a martyred little breath. "I shall just have to be patient with him."

Aunt Harriet interrupted them. "Jenny must be tired after her drive down from Viana, if you like I'll take her to her villa and we'll see you in the morning."

Rozalinda sulked prettily at the prospect of her party breaking up so early, wrapping her arm around Mary's shoulders and insisting that at least *she* would stay for a little longer. As I kissed Mary goodnight, I whispered:— "See you in the morning for a chat," and squeezed her hand. Our roles seemed to be reversing. Previously it had been Mary who had dispensed comfort and reassurance. Now it seemed to be my turn.

The breeze blowing in from the Atlantic had a refreshing bite to it after the perfume laden air of Rozalinda's villa. I linked my arm with Aunt Harriet's as we made our way in the moonlight down the shallow stone steps and out of the garden into the woods.

"Will you be able to find your way back all right. It's very dark."

"Phht, child, of course I will. I live here for nine months out of every twelve, I know every path in these woods like the back of my hand. Now let's cut out the chit-chat. Who is this young man you say you intend marrying?"

"His name is Jonathan Brown and he's English."

"You told everyone that at the dinner table," she said caustically. "Now tell me what he's *like*."

"He's … nice," I said inadequately.

"So are thousands. What's so special about this one?"

"You'll see when he arrives. He needs me and loves me and I'm happy, Aunt Harriet. Really and truly happy."

"Well, for that child I'm glad. It's about time you had your share of happiness." There was silence for a few minutes and then she said:– "Does he know?".

"No. Not yet." I saw her expression change and said quickly. "I was going to tell him on our last evening. I started to but he said we would have plenty of time to talk when he came here and that nothing I had done could change the way he felt about me."

"If he's a good man then it won't." Aunt Harriet said, but beneath the firmness I knew she was worrying that I was about to be hurt yet again.

"He *is* a good man, and everything is going to be all right. I know it is."

"I hope so, child. I really do hope so."

The pines thinned and the three villas gleamed in the moonlight. They were set in a rough triangle. Phil's the nearest and parallel with it the villa Miles was occupying, and some twenty-five yards behind them, mine. Aunt Harriet pushed open the door and switched on the light.

A large stone fireplace linked the two main downstairs rooms together. The floor was tiled and scattered with the same pretty rugs I had seen in Phil's villa. But here, instead of only two grand pianos and floor cushions for furnishings, were comfortable settees and deeply upholstered chairs in rich velvet and small, marble topped coffee tables. A scattering of softly shaded lamps had switched on simultaneously at Aunt Harriet's touch, giving the room a soft, welcoming glow.

"There's only one bedroom in this villa," Aunt Harriet said, leading the way into a beautifully equipped kitchen. "It isn't often in use, being the furthest away from Rozalinda's." A wrought iron spiral staircase led enticingly upstairs. While Aunt Harriet began making coffee I went

up, gasping with pleasure at the bedroom with its four
poster bed with white lace canopy and decadent looking
silk sheets. Through an open door I could see the bathroom
and a wealth of gold fittings. I ran back downstairs.

"It's super! Are all the villas as nice as this?"

"This," Aunt Harriet said dryly. "Is the most spartan.
Most of the furniture was taken out of Phil's at his request.
Rozalinda knew that without a piano she would never
persuade him to come here. Miles comes quite regularly
and so his villa has a lot of his personal possessions in it and
is never used by anyone else. Mary and Tom's villa is the one
guests usually have. Mine is next to it and so far Rozalinda
has left me its sole occupant."

"And you like it here?"

"Yes. When it's quiet."

"You mean when Rozalinda is away?"

"Rozalinda doesn't bother me and never has done."
Aunt Harriet said reprovingly. "I love her just as much as
you or Phil and you should have the commonsense to know
that. No, it's been Harold who has been making all the
commotion this last few days."

"*Harold*?"

"Him and Miles. I could hear them rowing the other
night."

"I can't imagine Harold rowing with anybody."

"Well, he has lately. Miles wants Rozalinda to sign a
contract for this film he's going to star in and we keep
getting frantic telephone calls from her agent in London,
but Rozalinda is adamant she isn't going to do it. Harold
has got himself quite steamed up about it. He's quite
insistent that Rozalinda needs a rest and that she is staying
on at Ofir until the end of the summer."

"Does she need a rest?"

Aunt Harriet nodded her head emphatically. "Yes. I've never known her nerves to be so bad. Which is why, of course, she's acting so stupidly."

"You mean flirting with Tom?"

Aunt Harriet nodded. "Though don't let that worry you, Jenny. I'm going to have a word with her about that tomorrow. If she knew she was hurting Mary she'd stop immediately. She just doesn't think."

"Then she should," I said, remembering the hurt on Mary's face.

Aunt Harriet patted my hand reprovingly. "You mustn't be hard on her, Jenny. She never had the advantages of a loving mother and father. I hate to say it but my youngest niece was totally selfish. She hardly ever spent any time with Rose at all. Which is why she was always round at my house and always wanting to be with you, Phil and Mary. And if it hadn't been for Mary she would have been left out altogether. You and Phil were sufficient unto yourselves. That little girl was intensely lonely and she has always been insecure. All Harold's money can't give her the security she needs. That's why she clings to you all so much. Underneath that veneer of sophisticated gaiety Rose is nothing but a frightened little girl."

"Frightened? I can understand that she's insecure. But she's nothing to be frightened of."

"No, she hasn't. Which is why it's puzzling." And Aunt Harriet abruptly took her cup and saucer back into the kitchen, saying:– "Have a good night's rest, Jenny. And don't forget. Phil's villa is the one to the right of you. Don't go mistakenly into Miles. I saw the way he was looking at you at the dinner table. I wouldn't fancy your chances if you did." She kissed me goodnight, closing the door behind her with the embarrassment of someone who has said more than they intended. I went slowly into the kitchen with my own cup and saucer.

The meek Harold rowing with forceful Miles. Tom making a fool of himself. Mary hurt. And Rozalinda frightened. It seemed I was the only person at the enclave without a problem.

Thank God, I thought sincerely as I slipped between the silken sheets. Thank God for Jonathan. And with the distant sound of the Atlantic breakers beating on the shore, reminding me again of our last night together, I ignored my tablets and fell into a deep and natural sleep.

I was woken by a soft tap at my bedroom door and before I could fully wake up a slip of a girl with thick dark hair tied back in a ponytail, came in with a breakfast tray of fresh coffee and rolls. It was just like being back in the hotel. She smiled shyly, placing the tray on my bedside table with a softly spoken "Obrigadoa."

"Obrigadoa," I said. "My name is Jenny, what is yours."

She stood hesitantly, not fully understanding. I smiled reassuringly, pointing to myself and saying again, "Jenny."

Her smile widened. "Joanna-Maria," she said, leaving the room with none of the nervousness with which she had entered.

I was still drinking my coffee when I heard Mary's voice downstairs, I swung my feet off the bed and called out:-

"Come up, Mary. I'm still having breakfast, ask Joanna for an extra cup."

She came in the room looking tired and drawn. She had never had any dress sense, now she was beginning to look positively dowdy. I poured her a coffee saying:- "You've no need to tell me, Mary. You're missing the children and want to go home."

"And how," she said fervently, sitting down on the bed. "We've been here ten days now and I really *do* miss the children. I wanted to see you, of course. I wouldn't have left till then. But now I know you're all right there doesn't seem to be much point in staying on."

"Then be firm about it. Tell Tom you want to go home."

"Tom," she said heavily, "is enjoying himself. He's being waited on hand and foot. He spends all day playing tennis or riding with Miles, and in the evenings Rozalinda flirts with him outrageously."

"Rozalinda flirts with everybody. Even Phil."

"But that doesn't mean Tom has to look at her with that stupid, besotted expression on his face, does it?" Mary's voice was beginning to crack. "And she *is* so beautiful. I'm sure Tom is going to be bored with me when we get back home ..." her voice broke completely and she began to cry. "I love him so much, Jenny. I couldn't bear it if he left me. I'd die, I know I would."

I put my arm round her saying firmly:– "The only thing that's wrong Mary, is that you're missing the children and it's high time you and Tom got back to them. Tom isn't in love with Rozalinda but she *is* his hostess, and if she comes on as strong as she did last night, he can't just turn his back on her."

"You really think that's all it is?" she said raising a tear streaked face.

"Yes," I said with certainty. "But you've been away from the children for nearly a fortnight. I think it's time you went back to Templar's Way."

"So do I," she said eagerly. "Only I didn't want to leave until you had arrived. I was beginning to think something was wrong ..."

I smiled. "There's nothing wrong. I'm perfectly well,

both physically, mentally and emotionally. Just you go back and tell Tom it's time to go home."

She wiped her eyes. "You're quite right. It's being without the children that's got me down. Rozalinda doesn't mean any harm and Tom would never be unfaithful to me ..."

"Then go and start packing," I said with a smile. "And don't take no for an answer."

"If we go now we won't be able to meet Jonathan."

"I'm marrying the man, Mary. You will have plenty of time to meet and get to know Jonathan once we're home in England."

"Will you be living in Templar's Way?"

"I don't know. I don't know whereabouts Jonathan lives. But wherever it is, we'll still see plenty of you."

She smiled. "I feel such a fool. Crying like that and thinking that Tom could be unfaithful ... you won't tell anyone will you, Jenny. I feel as if I've been disloyal to him."

"Don't be a goose. Of course I won't tell anyone." There was no-one to tell. Mary's expression the previous night had given away her thoughts to anyone interested enough to look. Aunt Harriet was probably giving Rozalinda a lecture about her behaviour right this very moment.

"I think Miles is going back to the States soon as well," Mary said reflectively. "That means there will only be Aunt Harriet, Phil and yourself here."

"And Jonathan."

"And Jonathan," she agreed smiling, her distress rationalised and dispensed with.

"That doesn't matter, does it? From what Phil has said Rozalinda doesn't want too much company."

"No, but she wants her *friends*." Mary said, her brow

puckering, "She practically had a nervous breakdown before Harold brought her out here."

"You're joking!"

"No. It was awful. No-one said anything to you because they didn't want to put any extra worry on to you, but now you're all right again and if you're staying on here, you'd better know what happened."

"Is that why Aunt Harriet is looking so ill?"

"Yes. Rozalinda was filming in the south of France. We weren't expecting to see her for at least another two months and then she was home. No make-up on, dark circles under her eyes and refusing to see anyone. She locked herself in the bedroom and stayed there. Aunt Harriet tried to talk her down but it was no use and then she rounded on Harold who was bumbling away about her having a touch of flu, not being quite herself, etc. Aunt Harriet said she wasn't about to be fooled by him and what had happened? She can be terribly intimidating when she wants to be. Harold just crumpled. Said Rozalinda had been receiving anonymous letters and that she wasn't able to stand the strain of it any longer. Aunt Harriet went back upstairs and couldn't get any answer from Rozalinda and she asked Harold to break the door down. He dithered as usual, saying Rozalinda wouldn't like it, but Aunt Harriet was terrifying. Said she knew her niece better than he apparently knew his wife and that if he didn't break the door down immediately she was going to telephone for the police."

"And?"

"She was unconscious. There was an empty bottle of sleeping tablets and a half drunk bottle of whisky and a note addressed to Harold."

"Good God ..." I stared at her stunned.

"Doctor Rogers came over and she was taken straight

into the local hospital. How it never leaked to the papers I'll never know. She was back home in twenty-four hours, saying it was all a silly accident. When she knew Harold had told Aunt Harriet and myself about the letters she was furious with him and when Aunt Harriet asked to look at one, said she destroyed them as soon as they came, and that they weren't important, and that what had happened was an accident. She'd had a few drinks, and mistakenly taken too many tablets."

"But Aunt Harriet doesn't believe that?"

"No and neither do I," Mary said frankly. "I was there and the bottle was empty. *And* there was the note."

"What did it say?"

Mary shrugged her shoulders. "Harold says it was simply to remind him that they were going out for dinner that evening. No-one else has seen it. Aunt Harriet asked to have a look at it whilst we were waiting at the hospital, but Harold said he'd thrown it away. It's never been seen since."

"Does Phil know all this?"

"No. He knows Rozalinda is here to rest and that her nerves are in a bad way, but that's all."

"What about Miles?"

"I shouldn't think so. He wants her to star in this new film with him. If he knew she'd been on the verge of suicide he'd be as eager for her to rest as everyone else is."

"Are they still having an affair?"

Mary's face clouded. "I don't know. If they are, they're being very discreet about it. And you would think Rozalinda would have confided in him about the letters. She hasn't I'm sure of that."

I poured myself another coffee, feeling badly in need of it.

"What on earth was in the letters that would drive a

person like Rozalinda to suicide? If it wasn't you telling me, Mary, I wouldn't believe it."

"I don't know. I think Aunt Harriet has a suspicion. She had a long talk with Rozalinda and she's the only person Rozalinda finds it impossible to lie to."

"Almost, but not quite," I said, remembering a couple of childhood incidents. "Are the letters still arriving?"

"Oh no," Mary looked shocked. "They couldn't be. No-one knows where she is."

"And if they did, Rozalinda wouldn't know about it. Not with both Harold and Aunt Harriet as watchdogs."

Mary began to look worried again. "Perhaps we should stay on. We're the only real friends she has ..."

"The children need you more than Rozalinda," I said, remembering only too clearly Tom's adoring attitude the previous night. The sooner Mary got Tom back to Templar's Way and family life the better.

"Did I tell you I'm teaching Helen to read?" Mary asked, her thoughts reverting to her children. "Timothy can walk quite steadily now. He's much more outgoing than Helen ..."

I gave the appropriate sounds of admiration, my thoughts elsewhere.

On letters so threatening that Rozalinda had attempted to take her own life. I would have been less than human if I hadn't wondered what they had contained.

Nine

"There's Tom now!" Mary said suddenly. "He's going for a walk on the beach. If I hurry I shall be able to catch him up."

"Then hurry. It will be a good opportunity for you to be alone together."

"Are you sure you don't mind? I could talk to Tom tonight ..."

"Don't be silly. Go now. I'll see you later."

"You are a love," she kissed me impulsively and scurried down the spiral staircase as if her life depended on it. I began to dress, rifling through my suitcase for tee-shirt and jeans. Then I walked out onto the tiny balcony and brushed my hair. In the distance I could see Mary scrambling down the sand dunes onto the beach, Tom so far away as to be unrecognisable. With her sturdy legs and plain woollen jumper and skirt, she looked remarkably like one of the local Portuguese women. I hoped Tom Farrar wasn't as bewitched by Rozalinda as he had appeared. If he was, and didn't agree to leave Ofir, he was a bigger fool than I would have thought possible.

"Hello! Anyone at home?" Miles called out from downstairs.

"Just a minute," I tried to keep the annoyance out of my voice. It seemed that villa doors were left permanently open and unlocked. No wonder Mary had run off so eagerly at the prospect of seeing her beloved Tom without unwelcome interruptions.

In the bright light of morning his smile was the same as it had been at the candle-lit dinner table. Warm and intimate, as if we shared a secret others didn't.

"I thought you might like to go riding. Rozalinda has four of her own stallions at the local stables behind the hotel."

"No. Thank you for the thought, but I haven't seen Rozalinda and the others for quite a long time. I've a lot of gossip to catch up on."

His eyebrows rose fractionally, the smile deepening. "That could take quite some time."

"Yes, I imagine it might," I said dryly.

He was blatantly handsome, with an inbuilt swagger that had served him very well in the small parts he had played in as pirate or cavalier. Even now, beneath the long curling hair, there was the glint of a small earring in his left ear. His last part in the film in which Rozalinda had starred, had been his biggest. The chemistry between them had flared on screen as well as off, with great financial success as far as the studio was concerned. I could well understand his anxiety that Rozalinda accepted the part of the Queen of Sheba. If another actress was chosen, the studio might very well reconsider Miles' suitability to be in it. His eyes were a startling blue, and bold. I turned my head away, the appraisal in them was undeniable. His voice had the lazy drawl that Rozalinda affected, though there was a mocking edge to Miles' voice that gave the listener the suspicion they were secretly being laughed at. All in all, I found him a disturbing companion.

"A coffee would go down very well," he said, the long, mobile mouth smiling as if he knew my thoughts. He sprawled comfortably on one of the sofas. It seemed I was destined for a long chat. Maria was upstairs, presumably making my bed, and I went still barefoot into the kitchen and switched the percolater on.

"What do you intend doing with yourself now?"

My hand faltered and I had to remind myself that Miles knew all about me. Had been at Phil's the night it had happened. I knew what his question meant and it didn't mean what was I going to do that morning, but with the rest of my life. A week ago I would have been unable to have answered. Now I said confidently. "I told you all last night. I'm getting married."

"And staying home to be a housewife?" he asked, suddenly at the kitchen doorway, very close and smelling of expensive after-shave.

"For a while, until ..." I couldn't finish the rest of the sentence. "What's so wrong in being a housewife anyway?"

He laughed. Nothing at all. Just that it seems a terrible waste."

Carefully I poured out two coffees and took the milk from the fridge, hearing the villa door close behind Joanna-Maria. "You must have been told before that you're terribly photogenic."

I knew what was coming: "And you think I could make it in films."

"Don't sound so cynical. Rozalinda is the biggest box office draw your country has today."

"I'm not Rozalinda. And I haven't the slightest desire to

live the kind of life Rozalinda does.''

"Why not? It would be far more interesting than being a housewife.''

"No. *You* think it would be.''

We went into the other room and sat down with our coffees.

"I know I don't have to tell a stunning looking girl that she's stunning looking. What's the problem?''

"There isn't one.'' I said, trying to keep my temper. "Just that I'm not made of the same sort of stuff as Rozalinda. If I'd wanted to go into films I could easily have done so. Goodness knows I've been asked often enough by Rozalinda's agent and friends. It's just not my scene. I was a nurse.''

"I know.''

The silence stretched uncomfortably and then he said:— "From what Harriet says I gather you don't feel you can return to it.''

I put my cup down. "I don't like enquiries about my personal life.''

"Jenny,'' his hand closed over mine. "Don't forget I know what you've been through. We haven't been talking about you. I simply asked her if she thought you would be open to an offer. This new film has a superb opening for a new actress and I think I could get it for you.''

I thought Miles had a very inflated idea of his own importance, but restrained myself from saying so. Instead I said. "I'm not an actress, so let's forget it.''

"Neither is Rozalinda,'' he said dryly. I looked at him. If they *were* still having an affair it was certainly not running very smoothly. Or perhaps Miles was a better actor than I had given him credit for. He dismissed Rozalinda with a shrug of his shoulders. "Were you serious last night about this man you met at the Santa Luzia or were you just throwing a line?"

"No. I was serious."

He raised his eyebrows and drawled even slower. "Marrying someone you've known only a week? Surely you're being a little reckless."

"Maybe?"

He laughed huskily. "I always thought there was more to you than meets the eye. That night at Phil's party ... only you weren't interested."

He put his cup down. "Maybe you'd be interested now. We could have a lot of fun in a week." And before I even understood what he meant, he had my wrists pinned fiercely behind my back, his weight on top of me, his mouth hard on mine. I struggled fiercely, but the more I tried to wriggle free, the more forceful he became. As his tongue forced its way into my mouth, Phil said leisurely:–

"Would you like me to come back later, Jennifer?"

Miles leapt to his feet, looking at Phil as if he would like to have murdered him. I gasped for air and pushed myself upright. Phil sauntered over to me, his long fingers clenched so that the knuckles were white.

"I didn't know you two were on such friendly terms."

"We're not," I said hastily. "Miles misunderstood."

He glared at Phil and then, his jaw clenched tight, pushed roughly past Phil, slamming the door behind him.

"Thank goodness you came in when you did," I said with a shaky laugh.

"Really? I thought perhaps my timing was out." His knuckles were still clenched and he wasn't looking at me..

"Oh Phil, come off it. You can't imagine I encouraged him!"

"Why not. I understand he's devastating where women

are concerned. Rozalinda thinks so anyway. Or did."

"*For the hundredth time I am not Rozalinda!*"

Phil's face crumpled. He turned to me, holding me close against his chest, his head lowered onto my shoulder.

"I'm sorry, Jennifer. I didn't mean it. It was just coming and seeing the two of you like that ..."

I patted his back. "Even you must have seen I wasn't being exactly co-operative."

"It didn't register. Only the fact that he was making love to you."

I drew away from him with a smile. "I shouldn't imagine Miles knows what love is about."

"I should have hit him," Phil said, looking so fierce and unlike himself that I laughed.

"I'm glad you didn't. It wasn't necessary. Did you see the way he left? I don't think he's likely to bother me again."

"I shouldn't think he'll even speak to you," Phil agreed, his good humour regained. "I came over to see if you would like to go riding?"

I forgot that I wanted to talk to both Aunt Harriet and Rozalinda.

"I'd love to."

There was no sign of Miles as we walked past his villa and onto the pine needled track that led through the woods to the stables, and if he could hear us laughing, neither of us cared.

Ten

There was no sign of Mary and Tom as the horses thundered over the firm sand. We reined in at the headland, the Atlantic breeze blowing fresh and clean against our faces, the horses snorting and stamping, eager to gallop further.

"Want to go on?" Phil shouted across to me.

I shook my head. "I want to see Aunt Harriet. And Rozalinda."

"Rozalinda's incommunicado."

"What do you mean?"

"I mean I went over there earlier on and Harold was in a fine old state. Apparently Miles upset her more than we realised last night. If she doesn't take the part she's open to litigation."

"Why?"

"Contracts. It's more than my tiny mind can take in. When she signed on with the studio she promised to accept the next two parts they offered her. The first a blockbuster and the last one is breaking all records. Naturally they want her in their Queen of Sheba epic *and* want her to sign a fresh contract, only Rozalinda isn't playing."

"Isn't it about time Harold told her agent how ill Rozalinda has been?"

I had forgotten Phil didn't know about her suicide attempt. He said mildly:– "I should hardly call Rozalinda's stubbornness and tantrums being ill. We'll go back and you can see her yourself ... if she'll let you in."

It was Harold who opened the door to me. His genial face was haggard with lack of sleep, dark circles making the pouches under his eyes even more pronounced.

I walked firmly past him saying:– "I know all about Rozalinda and after what I've been through I should have thought you would have come to me for help before this."

"It, er, it crossed my mind, but then Harriet said you were still ill and I, er I didn't like to say anything. Rozalinda is dreadfully touchy about people knowing. Even family."

"Well that's understandable. It's hardly something you would shout from the rooftops. I know about the letters as well."

Harold cleared his throat unhappily. "Nothing to worry about, Jenny. A misunderstanding, er, a figment of the imagination ..."

"Harold, come off it. It's me you're talking to, Jenny. If you can't trust me, who can you trust?"

From the expression on Harold's face it seemed no-one. Not where Rozalinda was concerned. I took his arm, softening my voice. "Where is she? I want to help her. She did all she could for me last year and I haven't forgotten it. Let me have a word with her, Harold."

"You, er, really think you should?" Harold dithered. Torn between the chance of helping his wife and the fear of her wrath.

"I think I should. If she's as distressed as Mary and Aunt

Harriet have indicated, I think I will understand better than anyone else, don't you?''

Harold's eyes flickered nervously from the stairs to my face and back again. It seemed he was incapable of making a decision so I made it for him.

"I'm going up. Don't worry. If you want to do something practical you could be making some coffee.''

"Er, coffee ..." Harold repeated helplessly, watching with agonised eyes as I went up the marble steps towards the bedrooms. Upstairs all was quiet. I padded on thick carpeting past a couple of bedroom doors, pausing outside what seemed to be the master bedroom. Tentatively I knocked.

Rozalinda's voice, sharp with fear said:– "Who is it? Go away. *Go away!*"

"It's me. Jenny.''

There was a moment's silence and then her voice, dull and tired said again:– "Go away, Jenny.''

"No. I want to speak to you. Open the door Rozalinda.''

"Oh Jenny!" The door flung open and Rozalinda was in my arms, crying hysterically. I held her tightly, steering her back towards the bed, whispering words of comfort.

"Don't cry Rozalinda. It's all right. Everything is going to be all right.''

"It's not! You don't understand Jenny! Oh God!" she twisted away from me, her fists pounding the pillows frenziedly.

"I know that you tried to kill yourself," I said gently. "And about the letters. Surely you can tell me about them. I want to help you.''

"Why?" she rounded on me, streaks of mascara smearing her cheeks, her hair in a wild tangled knot. "Why should *you* help *me*?''

"Because I'm your cousin and because I love you."

Her face crumpled again, tears streaming down it. "Oh God Jenny, forgive me. I'm such a bitch. And I'm frightened. So frightened!" Her eyes were glazed with fear, her body shaking. She crouched on the bed, kneading the pillows with her hands, no resemblance at all to the butterfly creature of the previous night. Tears dripped onto the sheets, her nose ran uncaringly. I stared at her, appalled. There was no play acting now, only a terrified woman, no longer caring what she looked like. I moved to the dressing table with its vast array of cosmetics, searching for tissues and handing them to her. She clutched at them, making no attempt to use them, moaning over and over again:– "I'm frightened, Jenny. Oh God, I'm so *frightened*!"

"But why? What was in those letters? It can't be anything that could possibly shock me, Rose. Tell me and let me help."

She shook her head, her hair covering her face. "No ... No ... Oh please, Jenny, *Please*!"

Inadequately I held her close to me, her body shuddering with sobs, her nails digging painfully into my arms. "I wish I'd never done it Jenny, but I was scared and now ..."

"Yes?"

She shook her head soundlessly. "I can't, Jenny. I can't ..."

"Would it help if Harold told your agent how bad you were and convinced him you were unable to star as the Queen of Sheba?"

Her eyes were blank. She had genuinely forgotten about the film part. For over an hour I held her, until the storm of tears died down, leaving her tired and exhausted.

"Lay down and have a sleep."

"You won't let anyone see me, will you?" She said, strength surging back in her voice. "Promise me you won't let anyone see me? Miles mustn't let anyone know where I am ..."

"He won't. I promise. Try and sleep."

She lay down obediently and I pulled the silk sheets up around her naked shoulders, closing the blinds and plunging the room into shadow. When I turned round, her eyes were already closed, her energy spent. I stroked a tendril of hair away from her mouth and went quietly out of the room.

Harold was waiting anxiously downstairs:– "Is she all right?"

"No, she isn't. Has she seen a doctor?"

"She won't. She just wants to stay here but it's not helping. I thought after a couple of weeks, but ..." he waved his arms helplessly.

"Harold. Until you get rid of whatever it is that's frightening her so much, she'll never get better."

"Frightening her?" Harold tried to look bewildered and failed miserably.

"The letters that she's been receiving. Are they still coming?"

"I, er ..." he chewed his thumb nervously.

"Apart from Aunt Harriet I'm the only relative Rozalinda has. Now are you going to level with me or not."

"She wouldn't like it ..."

"She's not in any state to judge and all I want to do is help her. I can't if I don't know what it is that's making her so scared."

"I can't tell you."

For Harold, it was an amazingly decisive statement.

"Why not?" I said exasperatedly, "I'm her cousin and apart from Mary, the only friend she has. *What was in those letters?*"

"Harold is right," Aunt Harriet said from the doorway.

"He can't tell you Jenny because Rozalinda burnt them all, and we don't know ourselves what they contained."

"You mean they are no longer arriving?"

"No," they both said simultaneously.

I looked from Harold to Aunt Harriet, convinced they were lying. That Harold should lie came as no great surprise, but that Aunt Harriet should, silenced me completely.

"I think perhaps we'd better leave Harold to get some rest. He had a bad night last night."

"Yes, of course."

Harold wiped some beads of sweat off his forehead, seeing us out, his fingers rubbing nervously against his palms.

"So you still don't think I'm fully recovered?" I said to Aunt Harriet once the villa door had closed behind us and we were in the garden.

"On the contrary. I think you're looking remarkably well."

"Then why act as though I still have to be protected? Mary told me about the letters and that Rozalinda had tried to kill herself."

Aunt Harriet let out a deep sigh.

I put my arm around her. "It's stupid you taking on all this worry yourself. You've lost at least two stones in weight and it's useless to deny it. Surely I can help. I love Rozalinda too, you know."

"I know you do, Jenny." Her eyes were bright with unshed tears. "But I was telling you the truth in there. I don't know what it is that's made Rozalinda so afraid."

"But you have an idea?"

"No." Her voice was too sharp to be convincing.

"It can't be that bad, Aunt Harriet. Everyone knows

Rozalinda isn't faithful. Do the letters threaten to tell Harold? Is that what she's afraid of? Losing Harold?"

"No ... it's not that."

"Then what?"

But I was up against a blank wall. "I don't know. I don't want to know. A few weeks and she'll be her usual self again. Rozalinda has always been resilient. She'll get over it."

Her words lacked conviction but it was obviously useless to continue questioning her.

"Would you like a drive out in the car?" I asked, changing the subject.

"No thank you, child. I'll have a rest. I'll see you for dinner tonight. I think I'll ask Maria to serve it in my villa. There's plenty of room and under the circumstances it might be wisest."

Helplessy I watched her bird-like figure cross into the next garden and climb the winding shallow steps to her own front door. She didn't look back.

Tom Farrar was leaving Miles' villa as I wandered through the cool green of the pines in search of Phil. He smiled. "Hi there. I was wondering where you were hiding."

"I've been riding with Phil."

I wondered if he had agreed to leave Ofir. He looked happy enough about it if he had.

"Don't blame you. Superb horses Rozalinda has. I shall miss them."

My smile warmed. I'd been as mad as Mary to think he had been taken in by Rozalinda's flirtation.

"There's always the local riding stables."

"Yes. A bit of a come down though after this."

"I should imagine it would pall after a time. Aunt Harriet was saying you were doing very well lately."

"Business? Yes. We've had a good year. Exceptional in fact. I might even run to buying a villa down here myself."

I controlled my surprise. Aunt Harriet had said Tom Farrar was driving this year's E Type around Templar's Way, but I hadn't realised he was doing so well.

"Mary will like that. She'll be able to bring the children."

"Yes. She's been missing them. I must hurry on. I told her I'd be back in ten minutes and she tends to fret if I'm late. See you and Phil later." And with an infectious smile he was off, jogging eagerly back to Mary and home cooking. Feeling happier in my mind over at least one person at the enclave, I let myself into my own villa to find Phil busy tossing a salad, eggs all ready for omelettes.

"Did Rozalinda let you in?"

"Yes ..." it seemed unnatural not to be able to talk frankly to Phil, but until I had got Rozalinda's say so I hadn't the right to tell him about the suicide attempt or the letters.

"And what's the matter with her?"

"Overwork I think, let me do the omelettes Phil."

He moved over obligingly. "There's some fresh cakes in the bag. Joanna-Maria brought them over a few minutes ago on her way home."

I peeped in the paperbag to see an enticing array of cream filled pastries.

"I'm going to have no figure left by the time I leave here."

"Nonsense," he said, apparently concentrating very hard on his salad. "You have a superb figure."

"I never thought you'd noticed," I said banteringly.

He put his fork and spoon down. "You would be surprised at some of the things I notice, Jennifer. Perhaps I should have told you before." And with his cheeks more flushed than usual, he picked up the salad bowl and carried it into the dining-room, leaving me staring with astonishment after him.

Eleven

Dinner that night was surprisingly relaxed. Aunt Harriet presided, looking much better after her rest, and happy to be playing hostess in her own villa. Mary had said happily :–

"Tom was so understanding about my wanting to go back to the children. It made me feel so selfish, I said we would stay on until Jonathan arrives and leave then." Her eyes were sparkling and she had put on a dark green dress that suited her. They sat together at the dinner table, holding hands.

Miles greeted me as if nothing had happened. The intimacy had gone out of his smile, but I didn't regret that.

Phil sat on my other side. He was quiet, but that wasn't unusual when he was in company. I had promised to go back to his villa after dinner and listen while he played a new piece by a young British composer. Even Harold looked more relaxed. Rozalinda, he had explained, had a migraine and wouldn't be joining us. Everyone had murmured appropriate words of sympathy and Harold had sat down beside Mary, leaving Aunt Harriet to preside alone. She looked quite grand that evening, wearing a black silk dress and two heavy ropes of pearls, thick white hair waving back off her face into a high chignon. In the soft candle-light it seemed impossible to believe that she was seventy-two.

"You're not going to forgive me for this, Jenny," Miles said suddenly. "There was a telephone call about a half hour ago and I'd forgotten all about it. Apparently your fiance will be down a little sooner than you had anticipated."

"When? What did he say?"

"He's coming sometime tomorrow if it's convenient. Naturally I said that it was."

I felt my cheeks flush and didn't care.

"Isn't that super!" Mary said enthusiastically, half her happiness for me and the other half for herself and an early reunion with Helen and Timothy.

"Hope he'll understand ... about Rozalinda not being well and all that ..." Harold said, worry flickering across his face.

"Of course he will. Please don't bother about that, Harold. I shall tell him Rozalinda has been overworking and isn't seeing anyone at the moment. Jonathan will understand."

"Yes," Miles said, wiping his mouth on his napkin. "I must have a talk with you after dinner, Harold. Can't go on like this for much longer."

Harold ummed and aahed uncomfortably. Aunt Harriet said:–

"I think you're right, Miles. It's only fair to tell you that Rozalinda is far more ill than we've let any of you think. I talked with Harold this afternoon and we think it's only fair to the rest of you to know the truth." She had everybody's undivided attention. "The last couple of years have been nothing but work for her. I'm afraid they've taken their toll and when she came back from France she had a nervous breakdown. Not a serious one. But bad enough for her to need the rest here. I'm afraid there's no way that she could begin filming again in a matter of weeks."

Miles put his wine glass down. "I see. And this was brought on solely by overwork?"

"Of course."

Miles drummed his fingers on the table thoughtfully. "She wouldn't by any chance have been receiving anonymous letters would she?"

"I say, old man ..." Harold began but Aunt Harriet's voice cut across him.

"Why should you think that."

Miles leaned back in his chair. "Only that it's a shame you didn't tell me if she had. There's been a spate of them. Marisa Clavering had months of them, and Danella St John is still getting them."

"You mean Rozalinda isn't the only one?" Harold asked unbelievingly.

"No. They're rife. Though of course the people receiving them don't go out of their way to talk about it. No truth in the vicious things of course. The Claverings employed private detectives and they soon stopped."

"You mean they found out who was sending them?"

"No, but when it was obvious they might do, the letters stopped. My advice to you is hand them all over to a private detective. God knows you can afford the best. That will soon put an end to them."

Harold looked so relieved it was pathetic. "Everyone getting them ... unbelievable, eh? Must hurry over and tell Rozalinda ..."

Aunt Harriet laid a restraining hand on his arm. "Not just now, Harold. She's fast asleep. Wait till morning."

Crestfallen, he sank back in his seat and it seemed ludicrous that it was because of his wealth that we were all there at all. He must have been a walk over for Rozalinda.

"So that's what all the fuss has been about," Phil said disinterestedly.

"She's gone through hell," Mary said with an unusual edge to her voice. "I sometimes wonder if you have any feelings, Phil."

"Oh, I have. Believe me, I have." He looked directly at me.

Miles poured himself another glass of wine. "Then I think our troubles are over, Harold. I can promise you that there will be no more letters. Not once the writer knows you're all set to flush him out."

"I thought anonymous letters were usually written by women," Mary interrupted.

"Her then." Miles amended equably.

Harold was looking flustered again. "Not as easy as that. Rozalinda put them all in the fire."

"Best place for them as well." Tom said with fervour.

"I shouldn't worry," Miles smiled reassuringly at his host. "The letters themselves aren't important. Whoever wrote them doesn't know Rozalinda has destroyed them, besides I doubt if your private detective would find the culprit. The Claverings didn't. But bring it out in the open and let him or her know you're no longer afraid and they'll soon stop. Takes all the fun out of it for the writer."

"You seem to be very experienced in the ways of poison pen writers," Phil said unpleasantly. It was the first time he had spoken to Miles all evening.

Miles laughed. "I am. Rozalinda is the third to be on the receiving end of them. I'm just cursing myself for a fool for not having suspected what was the matter long ago."

"Thank God," Harold said sincerely. "I told her in the beginning we should go to the police, but she wouldn't hear of it."

"I'm not surprised. Think of the sort of publicity it could have sparked off. The thought would have been enough to frighten anyone of Rozalinda's temperament."

"But I thought you just said Harold should hire a private detective and be quite open about the letters. If he does that it will leak to the press anyway," I protested.

"Not quite the same as a police investigation. Besides, when I said be open about it, I didn't mean hold a press conference. The writer will know soon enough without that."

I looked blank and he said. "I don't know what was in the letters Rozalinda received, but I do know what was in Marisa's and Danella's. Whoever wrote them was close enough to have put in details of truth amongst the rest of the garbage. The writer is someone on the inside of the film world who knows the girls well. Just let your friends know, Harold. That will be enough."

"*My friends*! Good grief, Miles, you can't imagine for one minute that any of Rozalinda's *friends* would do a foul thing like this?"

"That's the other thing I read about poison pen letters," Mary said thoughtfully. "They are nearly always written by someone close to the victim."

"How hideous," Tom looked sick.

"I don't think we need talk about it any further," Aunt Harriet said, beginning to pour the coffees. "What Miles has said has put our minds at rest and will reassure Rozalinda. Once she knows she isn't the only victim and that Marisa and Danella have received them as well, she will be able to see them in perspective. We must just feel sad that anyone should have such a sick mind as to send them in the first place."

She led the way into the spacious salon, the subject firmly closed. No-one lingered very long. Harold was itching to get back to Rozalinda, though Aunt Harriet made him promise he wouldn't wake her to tell her the news, but would wait until the morning.

Mary looked only too happy to leave, clutching Tom's arm like a love-sick schoolgirl, and Phil was eager to be off and get back to his piano. Only Miles seemed content to stay, nursing a large brandy and cigar. We left him with Aunt Harriet who seemed only too happy to talk to him and walked in silence back to Phil's villa.

The pine needles were soft underfoot, the moon rising high.

"You haven't changed your mind about listening to this new work of Tom Calloway's have you?"

"No, of course not. I can't think of anything nicer. You played a piece of his at your last concert, didn't you?"

"Yes. The man's a genius. Just listen to this."

I curled up obediently on the big cushions as Phil sat down at the piano. Whether Tom Calloway was a genius or not I wasn't competent enough to decide. His music was too sharp for my taste and it was hard to find any underlying melody. I would much rather have listened to Chopin or Liszt, but had no intention of admitting it to Phil. Besides, my mind was full of Jonathan, excitement growing in tight knots in my stomach. Tomorrow. Only hours away. I could taste his lips and feel his hands on my body and physically ached with longing.

Phil said exasperatedly:– "For the third time, Jennifer. Did you like it or not?"

"It was a beautiful piece of music, Phil. Would you mind

playing Chopin's Waltz in C sharp ..."

"Opus 64, number 2," Phil mimicked. "Have you ever bothered to count the number of times I've played this damn thing for you?"

"I don't care. It's beautiful."

For a second I thought he was going to say something else. Something about me. Then he turned abruptly to the piano and played the waltz with far more fervour than was necessary.

Twelve

I was up and dressed at six-o-clock the next morning. It was a beautiful day. A fishing boat bobbed precariously up and down far out at sea, visible one minute, the next hidden by giant crests of surf. The birds in the woods were in full song as I made my own coffee, leaving the villa before Joanna-Maria arrived. The sun was already bright but without any warmth. I pulled a cardigan around my shoulders and set off for the deserted beach. If he left Vigo after breakfast he could be here for lunch. Or perhaps he wouldn't arrive till dinner.

"Oh, hurry my love. Hurry!" I said aloud as I stood high on the top of the dunes, flinging my arms wide with happiness. Then I ran down the steep bank and onto the beach, slipping off my sandals and running stright into the icy waves that creamed on the sand. Walking into the breeze, my hair streaming back off my face, sandals slung around my neck, I walked on ankle deep in the swirling foam. Looking behind me I could see no sign of the villas or the hotel. Nothing but sea and sand and blue sky. I was so immersed in my own thoughts that I didn't notice the footprints at once. I turned to see where they had sprung from. Like myself he had run down the sand dunes and into the sea, and then had walked along on the beach leaving deep prints in the sand. There was no sign of him ahead. I left the icy coldness of the Atlantic and padded along beside them, wondering if they belonged to someone from the hotel, or if it was Miles or Tom who had risen early. The sand dunes were thick with waving grass and the bobbing heads of scarlet poppies. I was nearing the headland when he called out:–

"Good morning, Jenny Wren. You're up early."

"*Jonathan!*"

He was sitting with his back against the dunes, lazily pulling at a poppy.

"*Jonathan!*" I hurtled over the beach and into his arms. The poppy dropped from his fingers as he held me, the expression on his face changing. The laughter faded from his eyes to be replaced by a look suddenly serious and intent.

"You haven't changed, Jenny Wren. You are still as beautiful."

"Did you think I would change into an old hag overnight?"

"No. A lifetime couldn't do that to you," and he bent his head to mine.

His kiss held all the fire and passion of that first kiss outside the medieval walls of Valenca. It told me what I most wanted to know. That Jonathan loved me and that nothing had changed.

"I missed you, Jonathan."

He tilted my face to his. "I missed you too, Jenny Wren. I couldn't stay away any longer."

"Oh Jonathan," I clung closer to him, his heart beating against mine. Happy and safe and secure.

"Will you come back to England with me?" he asked.

"Yes. England. Africa. Anywhere."

He smiled. "An English wedding will suit me fine. Is May sixteenth too soon?"

"Three weeks?"

"I haven't been wasting my time since I last saw you." His eyes suddenly darkened and he held me away from him. "You haven't changed your mind, have you?"

"No. Three days would not be soon enough," and I wound my fingers in the thickness of his hair as he drew me into his arms, kissing me with such tenderness I thought I would die of joy.

A long time later, as we began to walk back in the direction of the villas, he said:–

"I've been married before, Jenny."

"I know. It doesn't matter."

"It mattered to me," he said quietly. "We weren't divorced. She died."

"I'm sorry ..." the words were painfully inadequate. He gripped my hand hard.

"I loved her very much and we were very happy. I thought it meant that I could never love again, but I was wrong. I love you, Jenny. You're no second best and never will be."

We stopped walking and he turned me to him, kissing me again, leaving no doubt in my mind.

I snuggled into his shoulder. "You'd better come back to my villa and we'll have breakfast. It will give me a chance to put you in the picture regarding the rest of the enclave's occupants."

"It's just your Aunt and your cousin and her husband, isn't it?"

"No. There's a girlfriend and her husband and another childhood friend there."

"Tell me over fresh coffee and toast. I'm starving. I haven't eaten since I left Vigo."

I opened the villa door, glad to see that Joanna-Maria had still not arrived. I wanted to make Jonathan's breakfast myself. Just having him there made the villa like home and not just another impersonal room. He stood behind me, arms around my waist, kissing the nape of my neck as I took cups and saucers from the cupboard and milk from the fridge.

"Are you always so affectionate? It could make my housework very difficult."

"Or impossible," he agreed, turning me round to face him. As his head bent to mine I stiffened.

"*Oh no!*"

"What is it?"

"The clan. They must have seen us walking back. They're arriving in full force."

Through the kitchen window I could see Aunt Harriet with Miles and Tom on either side of her, and Harold and Rozalinda a few yards behind. Rozalinda was waving, not to me, but in the direction of Miles' cottage. Simultaneously I heard the distinctive sound of Phil's door being slammed shut behind him.

"Damn," Jonathan said good-naturedly. "Have they no sense of timing?"

"Apparently not. You stay in the kitchen all ready to make your grand entrance. I'll go and let them in."

He let go of me reluctantly, squeezing my hand hard. There was no need for me to open the door, it was all ready opening. Phil was saying:– "What a bloody hour of the day to arrive," and Rozalinda pushed past him, radiant and beautiful showing no trace of the ravages of the previous day, saying "Where is he, Jenny? Aunt Harriet caught a glimpse of you both from her window," and then, letting go of me, asked coquetishly:— "He hasn't been here all *night*, darling, has he?"

"Don't talk such rot," Phil said bad-temperedly and she pouted, looking across to Tom for support. He gave it in a flashing smile, saying:— "Come on, Jenny. Where have you got him hidden?"

Before I could reply I heard the kitchen door open behind me and Jonathan entered the room.

I had a perfect view of the expression on all their faces. Aunt Harriet paled, her mouth opening noiselessly. Mary stared at him, bewildered. Tom, incredulous. Phil began to move towards me and then Rozalinda screamed and went on screaming until Harold grasped hold of her and shook her hard.

Stunned, I turned to Jonathan. "What is it? What's the matter?"

Phil had hold of my arm.

"I think you got his name wrong, Jennifer." And then, almost brutally, he said to Jonathan:— "This is Jennifer Harland."

Slowly Jonathan walked across the room towards me. I was vaguely aware that everyone else, apart from Phil, had instinctively moved backwards. Jonathan's face was dreadful. His expression one of such fury and grief that I thought I was going to faint. Then his hand came up and struck me across the face hard.

"*You bitch. You filthy, lying, murdering little bitch!*"

I couldn't breathe. My ears were drumming, and then I pitched forwards in a vortex of thundering blackness, to lie senselessly at his feet.

Thirteen

"Have a nice weekend," Sister Maynard called from her office as I went off duty.

"Thanks, I will." I put my head round the glass door of her office. "Little Kenny Barnes isn't too happy. Perhaps you could ask Nurse Rowse to keep a special eye on him."

"I will. It's always the same if his mother doesn't make the afternoon visiting."

I hurried across to the nurses' home and changed out of my staff nurse uniform and into sweater and jeans. Then I hurriedly threw my night things and the book I was reading into my bag and went out to my car. The Fiat was my pride and joy. The first thing I had ever bought myself. I settled myself happily behind the wheel and rolled down the drive and out onto the main road. It was a comfortable hour's run to Templar's Way and I judged I should be there about six-o-clock. It would give me plenty of time to talk to Aunt Harriet and catch up on the latest village news, and to have a bath and change in readiness for Phil's party.

Bromley High Street was relatively quiet as I cruised down it half an hour later. I turned right for Hayes, breathing a deep sigh of contentment as I sped across the common. From here on it was villages and open countryside. And home. Bluebells crammed the woods, the branches meeting above the narrow road, shadowing everything in a soft green. I plunged down a steep wooded hill, past the church I had been christened in and which still had original Norman foundations, and then crossed the valley and climbed up to the opposite hilltop where Templar's Way commanded magnificent views across the Weald.

The distant church bells chimed six as I drove past the 'Royal Oak' pub and rolled down the high hedged lane to Aunt Harriet's Tudor beamed cottage.

She was in the garden, secateurs in one hand, an armful of dahlias in the other.

"Jenny! You're lovely and early. I was just picking some flowers to take along to Phil's. Not that he'll notice them, but his cottage does always have a threadbare look of bachelorhood and I think the flowers help to soften it."

She took my arm. "It's going to be a lovely evening. Harold and Rozalinda flew back last week."

Beyond the silver trunks of the birch trees the Weald lay bathed in the golden rays of the dying sun. I sighed happily.

"It's lovely to be home. It seems an age since I was last here."

"Nonsense. It's only a month," Aunt Harriet said practically. "What are you doing for your holidays this year? Are you going with Jane again?"

"No, Jane got married at Christmas."

"So she did. I'd forgotten. Isn't it about time you started to think in that direction yourself?"

I laughed, "Who with? Phil?"

"Yes," she said, taking the smile off my face. "Who else?"

"I don't think Phil is ready to get married yet. And I'm sure I'm not."

"I think you're wrong about Phil. You know what they say. The spectator sees most of the game."

"Oh Aunt Harriet," I laughed and hugged her arm.

"Sometimes Jenny, I doubt your judgement," and with a reproving look she opened the cottage door and went into the kitchen to put the flowers in water.

"How is Rozalinda?"

"Fine. Miles is coming down. They are to star together in a new film. She seems very excited about it."

"Miles?"

"He had a small part in her last film. I believe this one is a little bigger. He's not the leading man, of course. They're still casting for that."

"I bet he's six feet tall and devastatingly handsome."

Aunt Harriet stopped arranging the flowers. "How did you know?"

"Because Rozalinda's men friends always are. I'm going for a bath now. What should I wear. Long or short?"

"Long I think. You know how Rozalinda likes to dress up." She picked up a rose and rammed it rather crossly next to an aster.

"I don't know why the hell I'm doing this," Phil said, as he let us into his tiny cottage at the far end of the village. "I must be mad."

"Don't be a spoil sport, Phil. You haven't had a party in ages."

"And I wouldn't be having one now if I had any sense. I'm glad you got here before anyone else." He gave me a brotherly kiss on the cheek. "Rozalinda and Harold are coming and bringing a host of pople."

"It will be fun. We haven't all been together for ages. How is Mary?"

"Fine. Full of the children. Timothy can walk now, which is apparently a stupendous achievement."

"Don't be such a bore, Phil. It is. For Mary."

He grinned. "Nice to have you home, Jennifer."

"Nice to be back."

Aunt Harriet displayed her flowers around the room, checking on the drink and the food that Phil had laid out buffet style in the kitchen.

"Satisfied?" he asked.

Her face softened as it always did when she looked at Phil. "The food looks beautiful. You'll make a very good husband, Phil."

"I'd make a lousy husband," he said good-naturedly, carefully avoiding my eyes.

The doorbell rang and he groaned. "Here we go. Once more into the breach ..."

It was Mary and Tom. I noticed with something of a shock that Mary's figure was beginning to thicken around the waist and hips, making her look several years older than she was. She looked vaguley preoccupied.

"I hope that girl who is baby sitting is reliable. We've never had her before and Helen has the beginnings of a cough. I gave her the number, but ..."

"Heavens, girl, we're only a hundred yards from home," her husband said in affectionate exasperation. "She has Phil's telephone number and she'll ring if she needs to. I don't intend to spend the evening running between here and home checking up on the baby-sitter!"

Mary looked sheepish, her fingers interlocking with his. "Sorry, darling I promise I won't spoil the evening by worrying."

"When does our star arrive?" Tom asked.

"Any minute now," Phil answered him as Rozalinda's tinkling laugh sounded from the garden.

The door opened and Rozalinda, a sapphire blue mink slung carelessly around her shoulders, a wisp of silk enhancing every curve, paused for us all to admire. Then, having made her entrance she dropped the mink onto the nearest chair and came towards me, arms outstretched.

"Jenny, darling. How absolutely *super*! I thought you were in London nursing the sick and dying!" her lips brushed my cheek, her heavy perfume suffocating me. "I must say you still *look* normal enough!"

"Because I am," I said placidly, too used to Rozalinda to take offence.

"God! *No-one* who *chooses* to be with old and ill people can be classed as *normal*!

"My oldest patient is twelve." I said dryly, but it fell on deaf ears.

"A very worthwhile profession," Harold mumbled from behind her, trying to catch hold of my hand and failing as Rozalinda swung wide once more, pushing him out of the way as if he were no more than a fly.

"Isn't Miles here yet? He said over the phone that he has the most *stupendous* news for me ..."

Harold finally succeeded in wriggling round his wife. He was thirty years older than her, balding and without any redeeming feature except his perpetual good humour and unswerving devotion.

"Nice to see you again, Jenny." The heavy pouches around his eyes made them almost invisible and his double chin had grown to swaying proportions since I had last seen him. "Mustn't take too much notice of Rozalinda's remarks. Doesn't mean them."

"No, Harold. I know that. How is everything?"

"Fine, fine. Rozalinda has just finished 'The Pretenders' in France and now she and Miles are to star in another film. It's a marvellous part for Rozalinda, but so far I'm keeping it as a surprise."

"I don't think I've met Miles."

"Grand chap ... devoted to Rozalinda." I looked over to where Rozalinda had trapped Phil in a corner, her body far closer to his than was necessary. Mary had told me that she thought it very bad of Rozalinda to have invited Miles to Templar's Way. Rozalinda had told her some months back that she was having an affair with him, and though Mary had come to accept Rozalinda's behaviour as unchangeable, she had been indignant that Rozalinda should have the nerve to bring her present lover to Templar's Way.

"I can't understand Harold," she whispered to me, as Harold threaded his way among more arriving guests. "He must *know*."

"Not about Miles, he doesn't. He thinks he's a grand chap."

Mary's little face looked tightly in Rozalinda's direction. "I don't understand her. I wouldn't be unfaithful to Tom if my life depended on it."

"No, I know you wouldn't," Mary's devotion to her husband was nearly as slavish as Harold's to Rozalinda.

"How are the children?"

"You must come round in the morning and see them. You'll never believe how Helen has grown ..."

The small cottage was packed now with friends of Phil's that I didn't know and friends of Rozalinda's. A tall, dark haired man, with a suntanned face and perfect set of teeth was coming towards us, a bottle of wine in his hand.

"Can I fill your glasses?"

"Miles, I don't think you've met Jenny, have you?"

"No, I certainly haven't." His dark eyes held mine admiringly.

"Jenny, Miles Sullivan. Jenny is Rozalinda's cousin."

He filled my glass, standing so close that his body brushed against mine.

"I've heard Rozalinda talk about you. She didn't tell me you were a beauty as well. Your bone structure is even better than Rozalinda's."

I moved a step backwards, away from the aroma of after-shave. "You're talking about me as if I were a horse."

He laughed. "No offence meant. You're just a very beautiful woman and it was the last thing I expected to find in this God-forsaken place. Apart from Rozalinda, of course."

"This God-foresaken place is my home. And Rozalinda's as well, though she isn't here very often now. It also happens to be one of the most beautiful villages in Kent." And I turned my back on him, not an easy thing to do in the crush that milled around us, and squeezed through the laughing, chattering bodies in search of Phil.

Rozalinda had her arm twisted tightly through his, the centre of a large, laughing circle. Tom was refilling her champagne glass, a bemused expression on his face. He had only met her a few times since he had married Mary and whereas to us she was Rose Lucas whom we had known all her life, to Tom she must have been the epitome of a film star, bringing to Templar's Way, however briefly, some of the glamour of the film world. I could feel someone's eyes on me and turned. Miles was staring across the room at me, a quizzical expression on his face, a smile hovering at the corners of his mouth as our eyes met. I felt myself flushing and quickly averted my head. Mary squeezed through the crush, nearly knocking my glass out of my hand.

"Do me a favour, Jenny. I can't get to Tom. Rozalinda is monopolising that corner of the room. I'm just slipping back to make sure everything is all right at home. I'll only be five minutes, but I don't want Tom to start to worry."

As a fresh gale of laughter came from Rozalinda's corner of the room I thought it highly unlikely that her absence would be missed. Seconds later the doorbell rang again, and Phil disentangled himself from Rozalinda to answer it. A crowd of people, some of whom I recognised as musician friends of Phil's crowded into the already crowded cottage. With them was a blonde-haired girl, holding an apprehensive child of eight or nine by the hand. Phil put his arm around her, steering her across to me. The little girl smiled shyly as Phil said:—

"Jennifer, this is Nanette Crown and her daughter, Sarah. I was hoping her husband John would be here as well, but apparently he flew to New York last night. Nanette, this is Jennifer Harland."

It seemed he had no reason to say any more about me. Nanette Crown held out her hand smiling warmly.

"How super to meet you at last. Phil is a great friend of ours and has told us lots about you."

"I hope it was respectable!"

"Very," she said laughing. "I used to be a nurse too. It was only a small hospital in the country, but very friendly and I still miss it."

"Can I get you a drink, Nanette?" Phil asked.

"A sherry, and is there any lemonade for Sarah?"

"Sure," he ruffled Sarah's shiny auburn curls and went in search of clean glasses.

"I shouldn't really have come," Nanette confided. "Not without John. But I wanted to see Rozalinda in the flesh. She's very beautiful, isn't she?"

I looked across to Rozalinda, slanting eyes flashing, her blue-black hair a velvet cloud, her dress showing every curve and ripple of her voluptuous body.

"Phil tells me you all grew up together."

"Rozalinda is my cousin, and Aunt Harriet unofficially adopted Phil when he was thirteen. We're all very close though we don't see too much of each other these days. Phil is still living in Templar's Way, when he's not travelling to concerts. I'm in London and Rozalinda is all over the world."

Phil returned with the drinks and there came a fresh banging at the door. With an exaggerated sigh he left us, stepping over the couples who had seated themselves in the hallway for lack of space and letting in a fresh influx of guests.

"John would have loved to have met her. He's a great admirer of hers. We saw her last film at Tunbridge Wells. Big night out," she said laughing. "She was terrific in it."

Close to I realised she was older than I had first thought, somewhere in her late twenties or early thirties. Straight, fine blonde hair hung from a centre parting to her shoulders. Her face was fine-boned with a delicately pointed chin and large grey eyes. Her hands as beautifully manicured as Rozalinda's.

"Why has your husband had to jet off suddenly to America?" I asked, immediately liking and feeling at ease with her.

"Oh, he lectures. This time he'll be away for three months. I hate it." The lovely grey eyes clouded. "Before Sarah was born I used to travel with him, but now she is at school it just isn't possible."

"She could go to boarding school," I suggested.

"Oh no!" I've only the one child. I want to have the pleasure of seeing her grow up." Her arm went instinctively around Sarah's slender shoulders.

She smiled merrily up at me. "Daddy won't be going away again. We're going to buy a farm and then daddy will be home all the time and we'll be able to have chickens and goats and all sorts of nice things."

"Yes, thank goodness." Nanette said with heartfelt relief. "This is the last parting. We're buying Hollings farm on the other side of the village and settling for the simple life. We've decided that money isn't worth a fig if you're not together."

"We used to scrump apples from old Hollings. He had a very nasty method of attack. He always used to keep buckets of icy rain water at the ready and if he caught us used to throw them over us with great enjoyment. We were always coming home soaked to the skin with feeble excuses of having fallen in the stream!"

She laughed. "It sounds like you had a happy childhood."

"We had, thanks to Aunt Harriet. Rozalinda's parents were always away from home and paid her very little attention so Aunt Harriet stepped in as substitute Mum, and my mother died when I was five and my father, who was the local doctor, when I was fifteen."

"No wonder you all love her so much. I've already found out for myself that she's a remarkable woman. When we first moved into the village last year, John was away and my automatic washer went berserk. There was scalding hot water pouring everywhere. I'm an absolute fool at anything like that and my first instinct was to race across to Harriet's. She had the whole thing sorted out in less than five minutes. Not only the flood stopped and the mess dried up, but she came back with a spanner and goodness knows what else and mended the thing. We've been close friends ever since. I was a town girl until I married John and rather apprehensive about living in a small village, but thanks to Harriet and Mary I don't think I've ever been so happy."

"Mary Farrar?"

"Yes. She's a sweetie. She'll look after Sarah anytime I have to go uptown. Whoever coined the phrase 'hearts of gold' had people like Mary in mind. She babysits for us as well when John is home. We like to catch up on our time together and go up to London to the theatre and concerts. I wish he had been here tonight. You would have got on well together."

"Mummy, do you think if I asked nicely she would sign her autograph for me?" Sarah asked, pulling out a small brown book from her dress pocket, her eyes feasting on Rozalinda.

Her mother looked across to where Rozalinda glittered and shone amid her admirers.

"She seems awfully busy at the moment darling ..."

"Nonsense," I took Sarah's eager little hand in mine. "Rozalinda loves children. She will be only too happy to sign your book."

Whether Rozalinda *did* love children or not I wasn't too sure, but certainly she had enough sense of occasion to realise what a pretty tableaux she made, bending down and kissing Sarah on the cheek and then signing her name with a flourish, whilst everyone stood back, smiling indulgently. I could almost read her mind regretting the fact that there was no press photographer to make capital of it.

"Gosh!" Sarah whispered reverently as we made our way back to her mother. "Were those *real* diamonds?"

"Every one," I said solemnly.

"Gosh," she breathed again, her face full of wonder.

"Satisfied?" her mother asked, laughing.

"She gave me a kiss *and* signed my book and Jenny says

that all those glittering things are *real* diamonds!"

"And it's long past your bed-time," Nanette said, bringing her daughter back to earth. She turned to me. "Would you like to call round tomorrow for coffee? We live at 'The White Cottage', overlooking the green."

"I'd love to," I said sincerely. The party had been worthwhile just to meet Nanette and Sarah. "About eleven?"

"Super. I can't see Phil anywhere. Would you say goodbye to him for me. Now we've seen Rozalinda in the flesh there isn't any reason to stay. It's impossible to talk above the music and this sort of party isn't really my scene. I'm more for tea and scones on the lawn!"

"Me too," we laughed at each other and she took Sarah firmly by the hand and began to squeeze her way through gyrating bodies to the front door.

I made my way with difficulty into the kitchen where Aunt Harriet was placidly making herself a cup of tea amid the blare of saxophone and guitar.

"Make that two please. Nanette should have stayed."

"She's a nice girl, isn't she? I'd forgotten you hadn't met her before. They moved in two months ago."

"She tells me they're going to buy the Hollings farm."

"Good." Aunt Harriet perched rather uncomfortably on a high stool. "Her husband is a brilliant man but away too much. He's in America or somewhere at the moment."

"Yes. She's missing him. They seem very happy."

"They are. When two people are in love it shows no matter how long they have been married."

As she spoke she was looking at Harold and she sighed.

"Not worrying about Rozalinda, are you?"

"No more than usual," she said, "I'm going to ask Phil to

play something on the piano. Claire de Lune would make a nice change from this row. As Phil began to play, Mary came in looking worried. By the frown lines beginning to etch themselves on her forehead, it was an increasingly permanent expression.

"Have you seen Tom anywhere? I can't find him."

"I'm not surprised in all this crush. Would you like some tea?" Aunt Harriet asked practically.

Mary looked longingly at the teapot and shook her head. "No. I'd better find Tom first. He must have missed me and be looking for me."

Aunt Harriet shook her head in fond exasperation as Mary hurried into the smoke filled room.

"It's Tom this and Tom that. Her life revolves around that man."

"You don't sound very approving."

"Well of course I approve. He is her husband after all. I'd worry far more if she treated him like Rozalinda does Harold. It's just that she's started fretting over the least thing and it's making her middle-aged before her time."

I put my cup down. "I've had enough for one night. I'm going back to the cottage for some sleep. Are you coming?"

"Not yet. I'll stay and help Phil clear up."

I kissed her on the cheek and edged my way to the front door. Phil was just finishing playing, the last notes dying amongst enthusiastic applause. There was no sign of Mary and Tom. I pulled the door open, breathing in the fresh night air with a sigh of relief. Like Nanette, parties weren't really my scene.

It was a dark night, the moon hidden by high banks of cloud. I eased the Fiat from between a Daimler and a sports car, waves of noise coming from the cottage behind me. It wouldn't make him unpopular with the rest of the villagers. His cottage was over a mile away from Templar's Way, cut off by thick woods, the only access a narrow winding lane, the trees plunging it into total blackness. I switched on my headlights and began to hum.

A giant oak that indicated the first of the sudden twists in the lane loomed up ghostly yellow in the beam of light. Still humming I rounded the high hedged bank and then screamed, swinging the wheel wildly over, ramming my foot hard on the brake. The car slammed into the tree, I was briefly aware of the shock of the impact, of searing pain and weight on my chest and legs and then blackness.

I regained consciousness briefly to a mass of headlights and a quiet commanding voice issuing instructions. I was lying in the middle of the road, my car a grotesque shape of smashed steel, nose on into the tree, the back wheels high in the air. I moved my head, searing pain making me cry out, straining to see amongst the dark shapes around me. Phil's familiar voice said "You're all right, Jennifer. You're all right. Keep still" and his tears fell onto my face, mixing with the stickiness of wet blood.

My eyes stared past him to a blanketed body. The head at a peculiar angle, the blonde hair shining softly in the darkness. By its side was a pathetically small mound covered with a raincoat, one tiny hand protruding, still clutching the tattered remains of a brown autograph book. The ambulancemen lifted me carefully into the ambulance, and agonising pain sent me mercifully back into unconsciousness.

Fourteen

I was unconscious for three days and when my eyes finally flickered open to the familiar sounds and sights of a hospital ward, Aunt Harriet was sitting beside me, her face haggard.

I knew even before I croaked the question.

"Nanette? Sarah?"

She shook her head, gripping my hand tight, silent tears coursing down her ravaged cheeks.

I stared blankly at the ceiling above me as a doctor and nurses came in answer to Aunt Harriet's summons. The pain in my head was blinding, I knew I was encased in plaster from my armpits to my thighs. I didn't even wonder what my injuries were. All I could see was Sarah's merry face asking. "Were those diamonds *real*?" and Nanette's face as she talked about her husband, saying, "This is the last parting. Money isn't worth a fig if you're not together," and the autograph book, its pages slowly flipping over in the night breeze as it lay in the blood stained lane.

"Oh God," I whispered, closing my eyes. "Oh dear, dear *God*."

People couldn't have been nicer. The hospital staff were kindness itself, Aunt Harriet and Phil seldom left my bedside. My room was a mass of the expensive flowers Rozalinda sent daily from the West Indies where she was filming. I had a sympathetic visit from my ward sister at St Thomas's, even the police were remarkably gentle in their questioning. None of it mattered. I was as dead inside as Nanette and Sarah, and I could remember nothing.

The charge was causing death by dangerous driving. Rozalinda insisted on paying for the best defence lawyer money could buy. I was totally uninterested. I didn't want a defence lawyer. What could a defence lawyer do? I had killed them both. Nothing could bring them back. And it was all my fault. I was allowed bail and spent it all in hospital, my physical self slowly recovering, my mental self slowly deteriorating.

I went through the trial like a zombie, remembering only brief words that my barrister said:

'Pleads guilty ... dark night ... road unlit ... no alcohol in the bloodstream ... had headlights full on ... on a bend ... victims wearing dark clothes ...'

I was given a suspended sentence and disqualified from driving for one year. Faceless people told me I was lucky, that I could go home, could forget. But I hadn't wanted a suspended sentence. I had wanted to be punished, and if the law didn't do it, then my own mind did. There was no going home. Instead I entered the Landau Clinic, neither knowing or caring who was paying for my private and prolonged treatment there. Nanette's husband had not been at the trial. He had come home briefly to bury his beloved wife and child and then returned immediately to America, leaving an agent to sell The White Cottage, the memories too painful for him to bear, Old Hollings farm was sold to strangers from London.

Days and weeks slipped by and I was totally oblivious. There was no emotion in me. I sat in a chair overlooking the carefully tended gardens of the clinic, my mind unable to come to grips with the enormity of what I had done.

It must have been the summer. Three months after I entered the clinic that I even became aware of Doctor McClure, my psychiatrist. From then on I began a painful and erratic improvement. It took a long time. When I was eventually discharged eighteen months had passed. And still I carried the nightmare with me. Until I met Jonathan.

Only the waiter had pronounced his name wrong. It wasn't Brown, it was Crown. And when Nanette had referred to her husband John, it had really been Jon. A loving abbreviation of Jonathan. And to Jonathan I had always been Jenny Wren. Nothing more. Not Miss Jennifer Harland who had caused the death of his wife and child by dangerous driving.

I lay staring at the ceiling in Aunt Harriet's bedroom. What was it Nanette had said? "I wish John had been here tonight. You would have got on well together" and I remembered the ecstasy of our lovemaking and then the nightmare of his face as he spat the words 'murdering little bitch' at me. The agony within me was more than I could endure. There was no-one else in the room, only the sound of voices downstairs. Slowly I reached for my handbag and my tablets and mechanically took one, two, three, four ... until my hand fell slackly to my side and the bottle was empty.

Fifteen

It was Phil who found me and subjected me to the ignominy of forcing salt water down my throat and making me sick.

"*You idiot! You absolute idiot!*"

I buried my face in a towel, dazedly wiping at my mouth, trying to focus properly.

"Do you mean to tell me you did this because of Crown? Don't I mean anything? Doesn't Aunt Harriet? Haven't you put us through enough already without making it worse?"

Dimly I registered that there were tears in his eyes as he carried me back into the bedroom, laying me on the bed and covering me with a sheet.

"Dear God, Jennifer ... promise me you won't do anything like this again. *Promise me!*"

I said dully. "I promise."

His hand gripped my shoulders his eyes pleading with mine. "Marry me, Jennifer. Please."

I shook my head. "It's no use, Phil. I love him."

"But it's over, Jennifer."

"I know. But it doesn't stop me loving him or being unable to love anyone else."

I covered his hand with mine. "Were you the friend who told Jonathan to come to Northern Portugal if he wanted peace and quiet?"

"Yes." He bent his head, a sigh racking his body. "I'm sorry, Jennifer."

"It isn't your fault, Phil."

He got up without speaking and left the room. I sank back against the pillows, my brain too fuzzy to think clearly. Thanks to Phil it seemed no-one else knew of my stupidity, but minutes later even this comfort was taken away from me.

Jonathan's voice said harshly:– "Drama seems to run in the family," and then there was the slamming of a door. I struggled out of the bed. He was going. I would never see him again. As I swayed at the top of the stairs, Aunt Harriet rushed upwards and caught hold of me.

"I must see Jonathan. I must speak to him before he leaves ..."

"He isn't leaving. He's staying in Miles' villa. The best place for you is bed," and very firmly she turned me round and led me back into the bedroom.

Like a child I allowed myself once more to be tucked up, saying dazedly:– "He's staying?"

"Yes," Aunt Harriet tried to sound her usual brisk self and failed. "You forget that he's a friend of Tom and Mary's. And myself. Rozalinda asked him if he would like to stay on for a few days and he said yes."

"I don't understand ..."

"Neither do I. Phil came downstairs like a man demented and punched Jonathan firmly and squarely on the jaw. Said you'd tried to kill yourself by taking an overdose."

I turned my head to the wall with a groan. "He also told

him what had happened after the accident. Your mental breakdown ... everything. And that you had no idea he was Nanette's widower."

"But Jonathan knew that!"

Aunt Harriet shook her head. "He said if this was an example of your sadistic humour then you were psychotic and should have been given life for murdering Nanette and Sarah."

I stared wildly at her, feeling mentally unhinged.

"He can't ... he couldn't think such a terrible thing. *I love him!*"

"He'll be more rational tomorrow and so will you. This whole holiday has turned into a nightmare."

Her skin was ash-grey.

"I'm sorry. It's all my fault. I should never have come."

"Nonsense. What happened between you and Jonathan couldn't have been helped. Other things can."

She looked suddenly old and frail as she sat on the edge of my bed.

"What is it? What's the matter?"

Tears brightened her eyes. "Rozalinda is having an affair with Tom."

The room see-sawed around me. "You can't know that. She's just flirting with him to make Miles jealous. Mary said Tom had agreed to go home."

Aunt Harriet said bleakly. "It was late last night. I couldn't sleep and I went for a walk in the woods. Rozalinda's Daimler was parked far off the track and I was fool enough to think some local boys had taken it for a joyride." She paused unable to go on, when she did, her voice was choked. "Like a fool I went over to it, I could tell someone was inside because the windows were steaming up ..."

"And it was Tom and Rozalinda?"

She nodded. "I couldn't believe it, couldn't believe that Rose could behave like that. She was laughing ..." She hugged her arms around her thin body. "They didn't hear or see me. A bomb could have gone off and neither of them would have noticed."

"Have you spoken to Rozalinda?"

"No ... I laid awake all night wondering what to say to her, what to do. Then Mary knocked and said Jonathan had arrived and dragged me over here. There's been no chance yet for me to speak to her."

"Then no-one else knows? Not Mary or Harold?"

"No, thank God."

"What are you going to do?"

She squared her shoulders with an effort. "I'm going to tell that young lady exactly what I think of her, and Tom Farrar too. I don't know which of them is most to blame. When I think of Mary and how she idolises him ..."

I remembered Mary's face the night of the party, her worry over Tom's whereabouts.

"You don't think it's something that's been going on for some time, do you?"

"Dear God, no. How could it?"

"It's just that Mary has been looking worried and unhappy for a long time now. Perhaps Rozalinda isn't the first."

"If she's ever suspected Tom of being unfaithful she's never let it show. But then Mary wouldn't"

"Do you think Miles is aware of what is going on?"

"Miles? Why should it matter to him?"

I remembered too late that Aunt Harriet hadn't known of Rozalinda's previous love affairs.

"No reason," I lied. It was no good. A dreadful look of weariness filled her eyes.

"Not Miles as well?"

My awkward silence confirmed her fear.

She rose unsteadily to her feet. "I'm too old, Jenny. Rozalinda has broken my heart. Don't you do it as well by doing anything stupid." Her eyes were on the empty bottle of tablets.

"No, Aunt Harriet. I promise."

She bent over and kissed me on the forehead. "I'm going back to my villa for a sleep. Afterwards, when I feel a little stronger, I shall speak to Rozalinda."

But afterwards was too late. By eight-o-clock, when Aunt Harriet knocked on Rozalinda's bedroom door and entered, Rozalinda was dead. Shot through the heart, Harold's pistol only feet away from her.

Sixteen

When I awoke it was just after mid-day and I could sense that the villa was empty. The events of the last few hours came back with sickening clarity. It was impossible to follow Aunt Harriet's advice and wait till the morning before speaking to Jonathan. If he was still at the enclave I had to speak to him at the earliest opportunity. Not to try to re-awaken the love he had briefly felt for me. I knew there was no hope of doing that. But I had to do what I had wanted to do ever since I had regained consciousness in the hospital. I had to tell Jonathan Crown that I was sorry. That there would never be a day in my life when I wouldn't grieve for Nanette and Sarah. And I had to say goodbye to him.

He had himself well in check. His eyes devoid of expression. His face a mask of tight control.

I said:– "I had to come ... I had to see you again ..."

A nervous tic appeared at the side of his jaw.

"After the accident, I wanted to see you, wanted to tell you then, but you had gone back to America ..."

"Tell me what?" His voice was curt and indifferent.

I said, knowing how agonisingly inadequate the words were and yet knowing no others:– "That I was sorry ..."

"Sorry!" His eyes blazed with sudden anger and hatred. "*Sorry*! You butcher my wife and child and have the insult to walk in here and say you're *sorry*!"

"But I *am*, Jonathan! I never saw them that night! I couldn't help it! Dear God, I'd been with them only minutes earlier. I know you've suffered, but I've suffered too! I've suffered the torments of hell since that night!"

It wasn't remotely what I had meant to say and when I had finished I was sobbing heartbrokenly. He said coldly, the surge of emotion once more icily controlled.

"You've said it now," and then, "I believe you."

Through a blur of tears I gazed across at him, wanting with every fibre of my being to take him in my arms, to comfort him, to love the hurt and the pain away. I said brokenly:—

"And I'm not sorry for what has happened this last week. I loved you, Jonathan. I love you now and I will always love you."

He made no move towards me. "I came to say goodbye."

His lips tightened even further and he swung round, his back to me. Blinded by tears I rushed out of the villa and slap into Phil.

With a strength I never suspected he possessed, he swung me up in his arms and back into my own villa. Silently he deposited me on a settee and began to make coffee in the kitchen while I cried until I could cry no longer.

Finally he said:— "If you want to leave in the morning I'll come with you."

"Thank you, Phil. I think it would be best if I did. If we all did."

"All?" he raised his eyebrows.

I said wearily. "Aunt Harriet discovered Rozalinda and Tom making love last night."

"And her eyes have finally been opened."

"Don't sound so harsh. There's a good side to Rozalinda as well."

"If there is she doesn't often show it."

"She paid for my barrister and for the fees at the clinic and my expenses in coming out here."

"Money," Phil said, shrugging her generosity to one side. "Why the hell had she to pick on Tom Farrar."

"Because you wouldn't play."

"Because what?" he asked incredulously.

I felt drained, no longer caring. "Mary told me ages ago that Rozalinda and Miles were having an affair. By her behaviour this last few days the affair is obviously over and being Rozalinda she needed another man to boost up her ego in front of Miles. She's really interested in you. Always has been. But you were your indifferent self and so it had to be Tom."

"Thank you," he said dryly. "So this mess is because I haven't fallen into bed with her."

I smiled wanly. "Yes."

He shook his head. "You're wrong, Jennifer. Things haven't been right with Tom and Mary for some time. Whether it's been Rozalinda or not I don't know. Whatever it is, my falling for Rozalinda wouldn't have helped the Farrar's marriage one jot and how long have you been under the impression that Rozalinda had designs on my manly virtue?"

"Since you were about five."

He smiled. "Then she's been wasting her time for nineteen years. There's only ever been you, Jennifer."

"Correction," I said gently. "There's only ever been your music."

"There's room for both."

I looked at him tenderly, knowing how much I loved him and knowing that it was the wrong sort of love.

"We've always been like brother and sister, Phil. It's too late to change now."

"You could do me a favour and think about it. I want to marry you, Jennifer."

"No ..." looking at him, hair tousled, eyes sincere it seemed impossible that he could be feeling an iota of the agony I was feeling at losing Jonathan. If he had then perhaps it would have awakened some response in me. I stood up wearily.

"I'm going for a walk, Phil. I want to be by myself for a while."

"Jennifer," he said warningly, rising to his feet.

"Don't worry, Phil. I'm not going to do anything stupid. What happened earlier was a temporary aberration. I'll see you at dinner."

Reluctantly he watched me as I walked down the shallow flight of moss covered steps that led through the garden into the woods. I made instinctively for the beach. Staring down from the top of the dunes to two sets of footprints that led to a sheltering bank of sand. The sand still bore the marks where our bodies had ploughed deep into it in the ecstasy of our lovemaking. So little time ago ... Tears blinded my eyes as I walked slowly to the spot, letting the sand run gently through my fingers. I don't know how long I stayed there. When at last I rose to my feet the breeze had taken on a cold edge and I was shivering. The beach was still deserted, but in the distance two figures walked from the depths of the pines towards the villas. Rozalinda's hair streamed away from her face in the wind and Jonathan had his head bent, as if listening intently. They were walking very close together. Another emotion seized hold of me. One I had never experienced before. Jealousy.

"Not Rozalinda," I whispered under my breath. "Anyone else, but please God, not Rozalinda ..."

I stood watching them as they walked slowly to the gates of the main villa, heads close together. Then on the wind came the faint tinkle of Rozalinda's laugh and she turned, going into the villa and leaving Jonathan standing at the gate.

My heart was pounding painfully in my chest, my throat dry as he turned, looking out to sea. Then, hands plunged deep into his pockets he began to climb down the dunes and across the windswept beach to where I stood.

He stopped three yards away. I licked my lips nervously, seeing by the set of his shoulders that the savagery of the morning had burnt itself out. At last he said:–

"Jenny, I'm sorry that I hit you. I'm sorry it had to end like this."

"Yes," I averted my face, unable to look at him, powerless to hide my longing.

"Phil told me what happened after ..., afterwards. We've both suffered, Jenny. I don't want us to part in anger."

I don't want us to part, I wanted to yell. Not now. Not ever! Instead I said with difficulty. "No ..."

He raised a hand as if to reach out and comfort me, and then stifled the impulse.

"It's no use, Jenny. There would always be the ghosts of Nanette and Sarah ... It's no use ..." I kept my head lowered, the tears falling ceaselessly as he turned on his heel and strode back over the sands and away from me.

No use. No use at all. I stared after him till he was out of sight, but he didn't look back. My legs felt incapable of movement. I stood on the lonely beach, feeling as if I would never have the strength to leave it.

"Hi there!"

Shaken out of my thoughts I turned my head. Tom stood on top of the dunes, waving. With sinking heart I saw him begin to scramble down and come towards me.

"Phew, it's a bit chilly now, isn't it? This old Atlantic breeze doesn't give you much of a chance to get a tan."

"It's still early in the year."

"Suppose so. Say, are you all right? You look as if you've been hit by a bus."

"I'm all right," I said flatly.

He looked sheepish. "Bloody silly thing for me to say under the circumstances. You must be feeling deathly. Would talking help?"

"No, Tom. I don't think it would."

He rubbed his hands together looking uncomfortable.

"I came down to borrow one of the boats and go for a row. It's a bit rough but I like it like that. Especially when I have something on my mind."

For the first time I managed to drag my tormented thoughts from my own problems to Tom's.

"Like Rozalinda?"

He stopped rubbing his hands and stared, his face paling. "How the hell would you know if it was?"

I shrugged. "We're a small community, Tom."

"Hell!"

The expression on his face was one of genuine anguish.

"Don't worry. It isn't common knowledge."

He looked sick. "I think I'll definitely go out for a row. Want to come? Nothing like it for getting things in perspective."

"Even murdering your lover's wife and child?" I said bitterly.

"Steady on, Jenny. You make it sound as if you did it on purpose. Let's get the boat."

The boat was a disused fishing boat, looking remarkably spartan to be Rozalinda's property. Together we heaved it down to the shore line and floated it. I raised my head, looking at the sea.

"It's pretty rough, Tom."

"It'll need to be with what I've got on my mind," he said darkly.

The rearing waves and thundering spray answered something deep in my own soul.

"You're right. I'll come with you."

"I'd seen a couple of fishing boats out early in the mornings and they had made rowing amidst the Atlantic swell seem comparatively simple. It took me all of three minutes to find out that it wasn't. Between each wave the boat pitched so low I thought it would never surface.

"Do you do this often?" I yelled over the thunder of the crashing surf.

"I've done it a couple of times lately."

"And has it helped?"

"Well it sure as hell doesn't give you much time to think of anything else until you've got where you want to be," Tom said with something of his old vitality.

He was still pulling strongly on the oars, water slopping over us with each pitch and fall of the boat.

"We're hardly dressed for it." I yelled back.

He grinned. "Another five minutes and we'll give her her head. You can see the whole of the enclave from here."

I turned. Behind us, a frightening distance away, was the

pure silver of the sands, and above them, surrounded by the
pinks and yellows of flowers, the villas and the pinewoods.
My eyes looked in vain for Jonathan.

Panting for breath, Tom, rested the oars, wiping the
sweat and the sea spray from his face. The boat continued
to plunge and rear wildly.

"Now. What did you mean back on the shore about me
having Rozalinda on my mind?"

I looked at him. It was obvious why Mary loved him so
much. His regular features and dark hair and eyes. His
careful grooming and perfectly fitted suits. He didn't look
like a boy from Templar's Way, which is what Mary must
have always imagined she would end up marrying.
Although they still lived there, Tom brought with him a
sophistication. He travelled daily to London to work. Often
he went abroad on business. To Mary it must have seemed
he was the epitome of the successful man. And he loved her.
Or so she thought.

"It's been fairly obvious that you're very attracted to
her."

"Half the men in the Western world are," he said with a
lop sided smile.

"But she isn't accessible to them. She is to you."

"You haven't been talking to Mary, have you?"

"No. Though she isn't happy, Tom."

He sighed and swore under his breath. We were silent for
a while, the waves roaring around us.

"So it's just a wild guess on your part?"

I shook my head. "Aunt Harriet knows."

"*Harriet!*"

He didn't ask how. Didn't bother to deny it, just sat with
shoulders slumped and his eyes unseeing.

"When you said you were coming out here to think, was it because you intend finishing the affair?"

With difficulty he dragged his eyes back to mine.

"I suppose so. God, I've been going to finish it even before it started. But she's like a magnet. I can't keep away from her. I've tried and I can't!"

"You'll have to if you want to keep Mary and the children."

He didn't answer and I said brutally. "You're not the first of Rozalinda's lovers and you won't be the last. Unless you come to your senses Tom you'll find yourself without a home and family and without a mistress as well. The nearest you'll get to Rozalinda will be a pound ticket at the local cinema."

He looked at me as if he hated me. Then he said "Okay. You're right. God damn it, I know you're right. But she's like a fever in my blood! Have you ever wanted someone so badly, Jenny? So badly that not being with them causes physical pain?" His face changed and he said:– "Don't look like that, Jenny. I was a fool. I shouldn't have said it. I was too busy thinking about Rozalinda to remember Crown."

The boat sank down into a deep, glistening green trough of water, rising precariously to be smashed down once more. I understood why Tom came out here. The savagery of the sea was a compliment to the savagery I felt inside.

"I saw him earlier on. Leaving the beach. Had he been speaking to you?"

"Yes."

"Well, that's a start. After this morning I thought he'd never speak to you again."

"He only came to say that it was no use. That it could

never be any use now. There would always be Nanette and
Sarah between us."

My voice sounded as wild as the waves. The concern on
Tom's face deepened. "He's right you know. It's been a
tragedy for both of you. Falling in love like that. Not
knowing. But it couldn't possibly work."

"No ..." the tears were falling and I didn't even bother to
wipe them away. "No. It couldn't possibly work."

"What will you do?" Tom's voice was worried. "You're
only just out of hospital and a shock like this ..."

"I'll stay with Aunt Harriet. What else is there to do?" I
laughed harshly, pushing the hair from my face. "Someone,
somewhere is having a hell of a joke at my expense!"

"Is there anything I can do, Jenny? Anything at all."

"Yes. You can sleep in your own bed instead of
Rozalinda's."

He looked as though I had slapped him.

"Anyone else Mary might forgive. But Rozalinda ... Stop
it before it's too late, Tom. You know nothing can come of
it."

"Women," he said, as he turned the boat round.
"Bloody, bloody women!"

It began to rain, and the small boat was so tossed and
buffetted that it was impossible to see if we were making
any headway at all to the shore. Tom's pent up emotions
were unleashed as he tried to master the boat and inch her
nearer and nearer the beach. I welcomed the cold and the
wet and the growing height of the waves. They were the
outward signs of the storm going on within me. I didn't care
much one way or the other if the boat ever reached dry
land.

"I was a bloody fool to have brought you out in this."

"You were a bloody fool to have come at all!" I yelled

back, as the luminous green waves crashed over our heads
and into the boat. I began to bail. A watery grave made no
difference to me in the mood I was in but it was obvious
Tom didn't share my thoughts. Besides, there was Mary
and little Helen and Timothy to think of. The small rowing
boat continually plunged, shook herself, hesitated and
plunged again. The rain drove in sheets between us, so that
I could no longer see Tom's face. He strained at the oars
and the pounding and crashing continued, the sky
darkening and a real storm bearing down on us. The only
thing in our favour was that the tide was coming in. If it had
been flowing the other way it would have been goodbye to
Portugal for good. The pounding and crashing continued,
occasionally through the driving rain I could see Tom's
muscles straining at the oars, and my back ached in my
sodden clothes as I bent and scooped, and bailed out, bent
and bailed ... Time seemed to stop. I saw again Nanette
and Sarah laughing and hand in hand. Saw Jonathan as he
had been that first night at the Santa Luzia. Remembered
so clearly that I could almost taste him, our lovemaking, his
eyes desirous, laughing, loving. Hating.

"Out!" Tom yelled over the sound of wind and waves.
For a crazy moment I thought the boat was sinking and
then saw only feet away the firm sand of the beach.
Obediently I jumped waist high into the freezing water and
helped him drag the boat high up on the beach. Then we
leaned, panting, against it.

Tom wiped sweat and sea from his face.

"I thought we'd had it then. I thought that was really it."

"You were magnificent, Tom. If it hadn't been for
you ..."

"I was the bloody fool who wanted to go out in the first
place. Never thought to check if a storm was brewing and

too much of a landlubber to tell the signs!"

"At least some good has come out of it."

He gasped for breath. "What?"

"I think you've made your mind up about Rozalinda."

He gulped in great lungfuls of air. "We're leaving at the end of the week. After that it's finished. I promise you." He draped his arm around my shoulders and staggering with weariness we slowly made our way towards the bank of the dunes.

"I don't mind telling you, Jenny. I thought we'd had it. I thought of Mary and the kids. It's not worth it. Nothing's worth it."

We were both too exhausted to speak more. Wearily we clambered up the bank and onto the path to the villas.

"Some fool," Tom said, "is going to ask us if we enjoyed our swim! Do you want me to see you back to your place?"

I shook my head. "I'm fine. Tom. A bit wet, but fine."

We laughed weakly. The water was still pouring off us, streaming from our hair into our eyes, leaving pools behind us as we walked.

"A hot bath," Tom gasped. "And a brandy. And Jenny ..."

"Yes,"

"Thanks for the advice."

"Don't mention it. Perhaps I should open a bureau for lonely hearts. I have enough experience." And with a wave I left him at the gateway to his villa and set off shivering violently for my own.

As I neared the villas I could hear music coming from Phil's. Loud, harsh music, totally out of character. I followed Tom's advice and whilst my bath was running poured myself a brandy, taking it back into the bathroom with me.

There was only tonight to get through. Tomorrow I would leave Ofir and never see Jonathan again. And what, I thought despairingly as I struggled out of my wet clothes and into the blissful heat of the bath, would that achieve? Like the ghosts of his wife and child, Jonathan would be with me forever.

At seven there was a brisk knocking on the door. I finished putting in an earring and went to open it.

Miles smiled at me. It was as if his unwelcome lovemaking that morning had never happened. "Glad to see you survived this morning's crisis. Hell, what a moment. I'm not surprised you passed out. Thought I'd leave you by yourself this afternoon to get over it."

He followed me back inside, helping himself to a scotch and soda.

"I must say Phil surprised me. He was the only one to keep his wits about him, and when he came back downstairs … wow!" he laughed. "He simply charged into the room and landed Crown one on the chin. I've never seen anything like it. I would never have cast our ascetic looking Phil as the knight in shining armour in a hundred years."

"Never assume," I said, putting in the other earring and thinking he must have a hide like an elephant.

"Too true. Seemed to bring Crown to his senses though. Phil was frothing with rage. Yelled at him that the accident was not your fault, that you'd been in a mental home for eighteen months after it suffering from unreasonable guilt and that if Crown thought he was going to drive you back there he'd have him to contend with. Even Rozalinda was speechless. He said you'd just tried to kill yourself, which I take it was poetic licence on Phil's part, and told Crown to get the hell out of your life."

"Very exciting for all of you," I said dryly.

"I knew Phil was exaggerating and that you wouldn't be taking it so bad. After all, you only knew the guy a week, and ..." he put his glass down. "At least it means you're free to other offers."

"No," I said forcefully. "I'm not. Come on, we're going to be late for dinner."

One thing I was finding out about Miles, he had a very short memory.

"I just thought you might need a shoulder to cry on."

"No. I've done all the crying I'm going to do." I switched off the lights and closed the villa door behind me.

He fell into step beside me his handsome face sulky. We walked over the sandy track towards the bright lights of Rozalinda's villa.

He said suddenly. "Let's leave tomorrow together. We could go south to the Algarve. Forget Crown. Enjoy life a bit."

"I'd love to," I said bleakly. "But not with you."

His face tightened. "Okay, if that's the way you want it." And we continued the rest of the way in silence. I was scarcely aware of him. In another few minutes I would see Jonathan again ... for the last time.

Aunt Harriet opened the door to us. I tried to keep my eyes on her face and not in the far corner of the room where Jonathan's sun-gold hair and broad shoulders drew my eyes like a magnet.

"All right, darling?"

"Yes," I lied. "I'm fine Aunt Harriet. Please don't worry."

Mary was sat by the windows staring out towards the dark glitter of the Atlantic. I went over and sat next to her. Her eyes were full of unshed tears.

"Mary ..." I reached out to her, but before I could say

any more Harold was blustering into the room, his face flushed.

"Can't get a reply from Rozalinda's room ..." Aunt Harriet and Tom immediately stiffened, recalling the last time Rozalinda's door had been locked. The rest unaware of what it could mean, continued to make desultory conversation. Mary's hand gripped mine and she sucked in her breath.

"Don't panic so, Harold," Aunt Harriet said. "I'm not surprised she's overslept after the day we've had."

With Harold at her heels she hurried up the stairs. We could hear her rapping at the door, and as she received no answer, Tom, his face white, hurried after them, ignoring Mary's cry for him to stay.

"Rozalinda! Open this door at once!" Aunt Harriet commanded. There was no reply. By now even Phil and Miles were beginning to take a slight interest. Jonathan was too busy studiously avoiding me.

"Rozalinda! If you don't open the door immediately I shall ask Harold and Phil to break it down!"

"Can't we just get on with dinner and let her sulk?" Phil asked bad temperedly.

"Phil!" Aunt Harriet called, her voice beginning to rise hysterically. "Phil, come here and help Harold with this door." Without urgency he loped up the stairs followed by Mary and myself, our hands still clasped. The two men put their shoulders to the door, the hinges creaking. Then Jonathan pushed past me to help them and under their combined weight the door broke open, the three of them falling into the room.

It was Aunt Harriet who screamed first, clutching wild eyed at the door jamb.

"For Christ's sake!" Tom whispered.

"Rozalinda! *Rozalinda*!" Harold gasped, seizing the lifeless hand and clutching it to his face.

No-one suggested calling an ambulance. Rozalinda's chest was a mass of blood, her head hanging over the edge of the bed, mouth lolling open, eyes wide with a mixture of horror and surprise. The gun on the floor.

"Take the girls downstairs," Jonathan was saying to Phil. "For God's sake man, move!"

Dazedly Phil propelled us down the stairs. Mary was in a state of shock, allowing herself to be seated and obediently drinking the brandy Phil pushed into her hand. From upstairs came the wracked sound of Harold's sobs and then Jonathan and Phil came down, half carrying him.

"Look after him, Jenny. I'm telephoning for the police."

He sat on the settee clutching his chest and for a frightening moment I thought that he had had a heart attack. His face was grey, his breath coming in harsh gasps. I put a coat round his shoulders, turning as Aunt Harriet came slowly down the stairs.

She had always been bursting with energy now she looked every one of seventy-two years. Her cheeks were hollow, her eyes sunk deep. "Silly, silly girl," she whispered. "Oh, the silly, silly girl."

"Tea will be better than that," I said as Phil shakily poured more brandy, spilling it over the carpet. He sat down beside Aunt Harriet cradling her in his arms and I occupied myself with the mechanics of making tea, of caring for Mary and Aunt Harriet and Harold, of doing anything but think of Rozalinda's shattered body and of why she had done it.

"What are the police like here?" It was Miles. No longer self assured and sophisticated, but looking sick and frightened.

"The Policia Judiciaria," Jonathan said. "PJ for short and when it comes to traffic offences pretty fair. When it comes to murder I wouldn't like to guess."

Seventeen

"*Murder!*" I dropped the cup of tea I was carrying, hardly noticing the scalding heat as it seeped through my dress.

"Don't talk rot, Crown." Phil's face was still ashen by the sight he had seen upstairs.

"I'm not. You can't shoot yourself through the chest and then throw the gun a gentle three yards away afterwards."

Harold was crying like a child, his head buried in his hands, scarcely taking any notice of the conversation. Rozalinda was dead and that was all that was penetrating Harold's brain at the moment. Tom and Mary were sat, hands clasped, watching Jonathan with growing horror. Only Aunt Harriet seemed to have recovered some calm. Or perhaps it was simply that she was in a state of shock.

I said:– "You don't understand, Jonathan. Rozalinda made a suicide attempt before coming out here. She took an overdose and had to be admitted to hospital ..."

"She didn't try to kill herself this time," Jonathan insisted grimly. "Someone did it for her."

Miles had been the first to recover. He sat in a chair, a large brandy nursed in his hand, his eyes narrowed on Jonathan.

"Do I take it you have one of us in mind?"

"I don't have anyone in mind. I just think I should warn you what's going to happen when the police get here. There's going to be a murder enquiry."

"Murder?" Harold said, gazing across the room with befuddled eyes. "Murder?"

"It's all right, Harold." Aunt Harriet grasped his hand. It's just that we have to take everything into account."

His head sank back onto his hands, his shoulders beginning to heave once more.

"Why did Rozalinda make a suicide attempt?" It was Jonathan asking Aunt Harriet.

"There's no reason not to tell you now. She'd been receiving poison pen letters for quite some time. The pressure mounted up on her and ..."

"The police," Tom interrupted. "Shouldn't someone ring the police?"

Jonathan nodded and went across to the telephone. There was nothing to do but sit. Mary's face was stricken. Like Harold I don't think she had taken in what Jonathan had said.

We had all been at the room door. We had all seen the gun on the floor. There was something else as well. Something I couldn't bring to the fore-front of my mind.

Jonathan said:– "Try explaining a murder in Spanish to a Portuguese."

"I thought they spoke Spanish," Tom said naively.

"Portuguese," Jonathan said, pouring himself a drink and sitting down. Whether by accident or design he chose the chair the furthest away from mine.

Miles said to him. "If you insist on having a murder. You have to have a motive. I don't see one."

"What was in the letters?" Jonathan was again asking Aunt Harriet. Harold was lost to the world.

"I don't know. Neither does Harold. She burnt them all. Didn't tell us about them till she took the overdose."

"She must have given you some inkling."

"No ..."

I looked across at her. I had known her all my life and I knew that she was lying. She might not know what had been in the letters but she had come to her own conclusions and she wasn't going to tell. Even now.

For the first time I began to believe that what Jonathan had said was the truth. I tried to catch her eye and failed. She seemed to be avoiding looking at me as studiously as Jonathan was.

"But they'd stopped," Tom said bewildered. "That's why she came here. So that the sender wouldn't know where she was and would be unable to send any more."

"I don't think it would take a master mind to find out where she was," Jonathan said dryly.

"Perhaps not, but no letters addressed to Rozalinda have been given to her without Harold and Aunt Harriet vetting them first."

There was a short silence and then Aunt Harriet said:– "There was a letter upstairs. An anonymous one."

I remembered that Aunt Harriet had been the last one out of the bedroom.

"Let me have a look at it" Jonathan reached out his hand.

She shook her head. "I didn't touch it. I left it where it was for the police to examine."

Miles said tensely:– "Well, what did it say? Under the circumstances we've a right to know. Christ, another ten minutes and the whole lot of us could be arrested for murder."

"I think the police here are a little more subtle than that.

One murderer will be enough for them." It was Phil, and there was no hiding the dislike in his voice.

"It said only that the writer knew what was in the other letters."

Miles swore crudely. "You mean you've put us through all that for that superb piece of non-information?"

"I don't find it non-information at all. I'd say it brings a second person into it, wouldn't you?" and as Jonathan looked around at us all I felt indescribably cold.

Mary had begun to moan softly, her arms wrapped around her body, rocking herself gently to and fro. Tom had his arm around her, pulling her head onto his chest.

"Then it could have been suicide," I said. "If she knew someone had found out what has held her in fear for so long ..."

"That's what is so interesting. What did hold her in fear for so long? Who was it that was blackmailing her?"

"No-one was *blackmailing* her!" Phil protested. "She was receiving poison pen letters. It doesn't mean she was being blackmailed.

"I'd lay you a good bet on it," Jonathan said sombrely.

Aunt Harriet raised her head. "Jonathan is perfectly right. It had to be blackmail. I knew that a long time ago. But for what I don't know."

"Don't you, Aunt Harriet?" I asked, leaning forward beseechingly. "Don't you even have a suspicion?"

Her jaw was clenched, her eyes refusing to meet mine. "No."

Phil looked for the hundredth time at his watch. "The police are taking their time. Are you sure you made them understand what had happened?"

"Positively," Jonathan said. "This isn't London. Things will take a little longer."

"I've to be in Barbados in three days," Miles said defiantly.

"I shouldn't bank on making it," Jonathan said crushingly. "Not unless we get a sudden confession."

"Confessions ..." I stared round the room, "Are you saying *one of us* killed Rozalinda?"

"You must have been top of the form at school," Miles said sarcastically.

"Keep your ill timed witticisms to yourself Sullivan," Phil said, his lean body tensed as if he would spring at Miles if he spoke another word.

"A white charger and your outfit would be complete," Miles sneered.

Phil leapt forward and Jonathan, even quicker, sprang between them.

"Let's just cut out all the bad feeling for the time being. It won't do any of us any good."

Sulkily, Phil went back to his stance by the window, tapping the face of his watch impatiently.

"Jonathan, are you saying *one of us* was blackmailing her?"

"I don't know who was blackmailing her," he said without looking at me. "But I don't think she killed herself. I don't think whoever killed her was some passing maniac who just happened to look in. And the letter Harriet saw upstairs would seem to have certainly originated in the enclave. There wasn't an envelope with it, was there Harriet?"

"I don't know. I was too shocked to think ... to look ..."

We sat in the softly lit room, the dinner table next door still spread, the food untouched, the wine uncorked. Staring at each other and all wondering. The suspicion breeding in the room was palpable.

I closed my eyes. Rozalinda was, had, been my cousin. I had grown up with her and knew her as well as anybody. What would frighten her as the letters had frightened her? What hold could a blackmailer have over her? Not her extra-marital affairs. They wouldn't disturb her to the point of attempted suicide. So what? I could find no answer to the question so I mentally went on to the next one. If the blackmailing letters had been sent by one of the persons present who was the likeliest suspect?

Instinctively I thought of Miles. Not because he had a reason, but because he wasn't friend or family. And without helping it I remembered Tom saying gaily that he was thinking of buying a villa in Portugal himself and Aunt Harriet saying how well he was doing and that he was now driving an E-type Jaguar around Templar's Way. And there was Mary. From what Aunt Harriet had said she had been anxious for some time. Ageing prematurely. Had she known of the affair between her beloved husband and Rozalinda and fought it the only way she knew how? There was Phil. His remarks about Rozalinda had grown more scathing of late. And there was Aunt Harriet. She wasn't telling all she knew. I wondered if she had confronted Rozalinda as to what she had seen in the car the other night. If Rozalinda had lost control and grabbed the gun dramatically threatening to shoot herself and if Aunt Harriet had tried to wrest it off her and failed. ... The idea was too horrible to contemplate. That left Jonathan, but it couldn't possibly be Jonathan. And myself.

Everyone had fallen silent, occupied with the same grim thoughts. I leant my head back against the chair and closed my eyes, remembering Rozalinda when she had been seven or eight and we had played in the woods around Templar's Way. I remembered her kindness to me over the last eighteen months. How she had paid for my lawyer, my clinic fees, offering me the villa for as long as I wanted. And I began, at last, to cry.

Eighteen

After what seemed like an eternity the police arrived, grim-faced and speaking hardly any English. It was Jonathan who came to the rescue, talking in Spanish and explaining how the door had been locked and how they had had to break it down. When it came to removing Rozalinda's body from the villa Harold went to pieces completely, struggling against Jonathan and Tom to clasp her in his arms.

"Is this the husband?" the officer in charge asked unnecessarily.

"I have some tablets. Sleeping tablets," hurriedly Aunt Harriet rifled through her handbag.

"I think not. He will have to be questioned," and then, as Harold's sobs grew to a crescendo, "Were you all here at the time?"

"Yes."

"Then give the gentleman the tablets. Tomorrow will be time enough to talk to him."

A policeman came downstairs, the gun laying on a cloth in one hand, the letter in the other. With Jonathan acting as interpreter, the officer asked Harold.

"Is this your gun?"

Harold nodded. "I have a licence for it ... Oh God, I should never have kept it in the villa ... If I'd had any idea ..." he began to cry again.

"And this?" the officer held out the paper and read:–

'I know what was in the letters'

He lifted his eyes. "What letters? Who wrote this to your wife?"

Harold was unable to speak coherently. Aunt Harriet said:– "My niece had been receiving anonymous letters. they had upset the balance of her mind. I imagine whoever wrote this was obliquely responsible for her taking her life."

The officer stared down at her. "You think she took her own life? There was no suicide note."

"She had tried before. In London. The balance of her mind had been disturbed by the letters ..."

He looked slowly at us and then back at the gun. Any minute now, I thought. Any minute now he's going to tell her that she's wrong. That it was murder. Instead he said. "Under the circumstances I must ask you all to remain here for further questioning. Could I have your passports please."

Only Miles made a token protest.

"When did you last see your wife?" the officer asked Harold.

Harold struggled to collect his wits. "Lunchtime. I went to Oporto this afternoon. Didn't get back till after seven."

"And you didn't see your wife then?"

"No ... she sleeps a lot. Hasn't been well ...," tears engulfed him once more.

"I saw her about half past four," I said.

The officer turned. "Where?"

"At the villa. She'd been for a walk. I was on the beach and saw her return."

"I can corroborate that," Jonathan said. "I was with Rozalinda when Miss Harland saw us. We parted at the gate and then I went down to the beach to speak to Miss Harland."

"And you returned together?"

"No. I left Miss Harland still on the beach."

"And went where?"

"To the villa I share with Mr Sullivan."

"And Mr Sullivan was with you from that time to the time you arrived here for dinner?"

"No. Miles didn't get back to the villa till around six. He had been riding."

"And you," the officer turned to me. "Where did you go after Mr Crown left you on the beach?"

"I took a rowing boat out with Mr Farrar."

The officer glanced down at his notes. "Where did you meet Mr Farrar?"

"I was on the beach and he saw me and came down to meet me."

"From which direction?"

"From the villas."

"Which villa? His own or this one?"

I felt the heat rising within me. "I'm not sure." It had been Rozalinda's. I was sure of it.

"Then perhaps it is a matter to which you could give some thought. If I remember rightly the weather was not ideal for putting out to sea."

"No, it wasn't. It got very rough and we had great difficulty in getting back to shore."

"And got very wet?"

"Yes, of course."

"So all the clothes you were both wearing have now been washed?" he asked smoothly.

"Yes ..."

He turned to Tom. "And your clothes, Mr Farrar?"

Tom looked ill. "The sea-water had ruined my jeans and they were pretty old anyway. I threw them away."

"Where?" There was no denying the steel in the smooth voice.

Tom's face was scarlet. "In the incinerator."

The officer looked at him thoughtfully for a few minutes and then asked one of his men to go outside and empty the incinerators.

"When the pair of you had come back from your ... row. Where did you both go?"

"Tom went to his villa and I went back to mine. I had a bath and changed. Miles called for me and we walked over here together."

The officer was temporarily finished with me. Painstakingly Jonathan continued to interpret as he asked everyone else to account for their movements. It was two-o-clock in the morning before they left. The gun and letter were taken away for fingerprinting. No-one had seen Rozalinda after she had said goodbye to Jonathan. No-one knew who had written the letter found in her bedroom, or knew what the contents of the anonymous letters had been.

Tom mopped the sweat off his forehead as the officer and his men finally left. "Phew. What time do you think they'll be back?"

"Three or four hours," Jonathan said. "By then they'll have fingerprinted the gun."

"And will they take ours?" Mary asked in a whisper.

"Yes. But it will be for the best, Mary. It will soon be over." She shuddered, burying her head again on Tom's shoulder.

Jonathan poured himself a whisky. "And not one mention of murder."

"No, because she did it herself," Aunt Harriet said firmly.

"It wouldn't have been possible. Not unless someone had moved the gun afterwards."

Miles laughed harshly. "You mean she killed herself and someone who enjoys seeing the rest of us sweat moved it to make it look like murder?"

"I don't mean anything. I'm just stating a fact."

I said: "Did they take the key?"

Their faces were blank.

"The door was locked and if Rozalinda killed herself it must have been locked from the inside but I don't remember seeing a key."

"Not surprising after the sight you'd just seen," Phil said.

For the first time I saw Aunt Harriet begin to lose her steely control. "It must be in her room. The police will have taken it. They won't tell us everything they find or do. If they thought it was murder they would have said so!" She was shaking. "Dear Lord, anyone would think you *wanted* it to be murder!"

I put my arms round her. "Of course we don't. I shouldn't have mentioned it. It just struck me as funny that's all ..."

"It might be a good idea if you took a sleeping tablet yourself Harriet," Jonathan said. "We'll cover Harold with a coat and perhaps Tom would stay with him."

"Don't leave me!" Mary gasped. "Don't leave me, Tom!"

"Of course I won't leave you. But we can't leave Harold

alone tonight. We'll take him across to our villa."

Aunt Harriet said. "Thank goodness you were here, Jonathan. I don't know how we would have managed the police without you."

"I'm glad I was able to help."

For a brief second his eyes flickered across to me and I thought he was going to see me safely back to my villa, and then he said brusquely:– "You'd better take Jenny back, Phil."

Bleakly I turned to the door with Phil and Miles on either side of me. I had been a fool to think even for a fleeting moment that one tragedy could put another right. Rozalinda's death changed nothing between us.

Phil kissed me lightly on the forehead, standing outside until I had turned the key.

I didn't go to bed. Under the circumstances sleep was impossible. I sat in an armchair, poured myself a stiff whisky and tried to think. Fifteen minutes later there came a knock on the door.

Nineteen

"A brandy? A whisky?" I asked.

"A brandy." He smiled. "When did you find out?"

I swirled the ice around in my glass, saying carefully:–
"When I came here."

"How?"

"Rozalinda told me."

He sat opposite me, one leg swinging idly over the arm of
the chair. "That I find very hard to believe."

I shrugged. "Believe what you want. She was half out of
her mind with fear. She thought that by telling me I could
help."

He threw his head back and laughed. "Christ! You did
that all right!" Then he leaned forward, his eyes holding
mine, a strange light in them. "Did you enjoy doing it?"

"Doing what?"

"Killing her."

"She killed herself."

"And threw the gun three feet across the floor
afterwards? She was killed, and you did it, didn't you? It
must have given you great pleasure after what she did to
you."

I drank the remainder of my whisky. "Yes," I agreed at last. "Great pleasure."

"You realize you killed the goose laying my golden eggs?"

"I thought you'd done it for revenge, not money."

"I did. In the beginning. Then I couldn't care less who she slept with."

"So as you can't blackmail me for money, what are you going to blackmail me for?"

He leaned back. "I don't know. Not yet. But it's a nice feeling. Having someone in your power."

"I'm glad you're enjoying it," I crossed the room and poured myself another drink. "Did you know about Rozalinda immediately?"

"Yes. I knew she'd arranged to meet that insignificant bastard somewhere and I followed her. I hadn't counted on her taking the car though. By the time I reached the lane she was already on her way back, driving like a bat out of hell."

My mouth was very dry, the blood pounding in my ears. "What did you do? Follow her back in?"

"No. I figured the boy-friend was still out there so I went to meet him. Offer a few words of kindly advice. Both the woman and the kid were dead. She must have lammed into them at about fifty."

The room was reeling, my voice seemed to come from a far distance as I struggled to say calmly:—

"And she never knew it was you who was blackmailing her?"

"You know that yourself."

"Yes ... but she must have known it was someone who was at the party that night."

"Obviously. But she was too pea-brained to work it out."

I sipped at the whisky, desperately trying to re-arrange the pieces in the jigsaw.

"I think we can seal our new arrangement now."

I stared, uncomprehending. The leg still swung idly, but the expression in his eyes was one that sent chills down my spine.

"Take your skirt off first and then, very slowly, your sweater."

"No ..."

He laughed softly. "Don't be a fool. Do you want me to tell the police you murdered Rozalinda?"

"If you do I'll tell them you blackmailed her."

"Which they won't believe. I'm completely in the clear. But you're not. And neither is Crown."

"What can you do to Jonathan?" Fear choked my voice to a whisper.

"Thanks to your ill starred love affair, what could be more obvious than on finding out who really killed his wife and child, he helped you murder Rozalinda. Or even did it himself."

"No ..." I shrank back in the chair. "You wouldn't ..."

"Believe me, I would," he said softly. "Now take off your clothes ..."

"No ..." he was coming towards me. "You can't blackmail me. I didn't do it!"

He halted, the smile wiped from his face. I said frantically:–

"You assumed I had and I let you because I wanted you to talk. I never knew what was in the letter till you told me tonight. I never knew I hadn't killed them!"

I expected him to hit me, instead the smile slowly returned. "Then if you didn't murder her, Crown did. If you're a good girl I won't tell the police ..."

Jonathan, of course, it was Jonathan. "You promise? I asked hoarsely, "You promise not to tell them it was Jonathan ..."

"If you do what I want," he said pleasantly. "Now take off your clothes. One by one and very slowly."

Jonathan. Jonathan had murdered Rozalinda. My brain whirled. Had it only been revenge for Nanette and Sarah? Or had it been for me as well? Whatever the reason I had to prevent Miles telling the police. No-one else knew what Rozalinda had done. No-one else could possibly suspect Jonathan. If I did what Miles asked ... I knew, even as my skirt fell to the floor, that Miles was happy not to tell the police. That in Jonathan he had another victim with enough money to make blackmail worthwhile. But I had to keep him happy till the police enquiries were over. I couldn't risk upsetting him. Couldn't risk Jonathan's arrest, whatever the cost.

I stood in the lamplight, Miles eyes lingering over my legs, desperately trying to think of a way of stalling him.

"You could come with me tomorrow when I leave ..."

He shook his head. "I'm not waiting for tomorrow. Now your sweater."

Hands damp with sweat I lifted my sweater over my head, letting it fall to the floor to join my skirt in a crumpled heap.

"What about a drink first, Miles? Let's have a brandy ... a whisky ..."

He laughed. "You really are scared, aren't you? What's the matter, Jenny. Is this your first time?"

"Yes ..."

The faint surge of hope soon died. His eyes gleamed. "All the more exciting. Now your bra."

Somewhere a door creaked. Or was it my imagination as he began to whisper the things he was going to do to me. The things he would make me do. The sound came again and this time I knew it had not been my imagination. Behind his chair, out of range of the lamplight, I sensed someone's presence.

I closed my eyes, unable to bear the sight of his eyes on my half naked body. Please God ... let it be Phil. Let it be Aunt Harriet. Let it be anyone as long as this humiliation stops.

"Now your panties ..."

There was no sound. No help coming. I remained motionless.

"If you don't, Jonathan will be arrested before morning." His voice was quite pleasant. As if he were saying what a nice day it was. How fortunate that the weather had changed.

I began to cry silently, my fingers sliding slowly to my hips, then slower still as I struggled to keep my eyes on his face and not on the figure emerging from the shadows and approaching the back of Miles' chair. Not until the strong arm had jack-knifed down, wrenching his head back, did I tear my eyes away and scream.

With enormous effort Miles' flailing arms caught the back of Jonathan's head, heaving him bodily over the chair, breaking Jonathan's grip, both of them crashing to the floor at my feet. Miles' fist landed punch after punch on Jonathan's jaw whilst Jonathan kicked upwards with his legs sending Miles sprawling, leaping down on top of him, his hands closing around his throat.

"*No! Jonathan! No!*"

But Jonathan's eyes were glazed as he panted and

struggled to squeeze the life from Miles.

"*Bastard!*" he gasped, his muscles straining. "You foul mouthed, filthy *bastard!*"

I grabbed my sweater, struggling into it as I ran out of the villa across to Phil's, hammering hysterically on the door.

"What the ... *Jennifer!*" Then he heard the grunting struggle and began running barefoot, shouting for help at the top of his voice.

Miles was half senseless as Phil strained to pull Jonathan off him and Aunt Harriet, Tom and Mary rushed half dressed into the room.

I was only half aware of Mary as she silently handed me my skirt and as Tom and Aunt Harriet poured water over Miles. I threw myself at Jonathan, holding his bleeding face between my hands, saying urgently:—

"Don't tell them! Dear God, don't tell them!"

His arm came down around my body, hugging me towards him.

"It's all right, Jenny Wren. It's all right."

I was still crying. "It isn't. Oh Jonathan, they'll take you away ..."

"No they won't my love. Nothing will ever take me away from you again."

Miles was struggling for breath, Tom and Phil hesitantly at either side of him. Ready to seize him if he moved and not knowing why.

Aunt Harriet, satisfied that Miles would live, sat down heavily and with remarkable presence of mind said simply:—"What happened?"

"Nothing ..." I said frantically. "Miles was making a pass at me and ..."

"Some pass," Phil said between clenched teeth, looking at the bra lying on the rug.

"He was blackmailing her," Jonathan cut in. "He forced her to undress and then ..." he looked down at me, his eyes dark. "And then I came in."

"Liar!" Miles yelled. "He was trying to kill me!"

"Why?" Aunt Harriet's voice was like ice.

"Because he murdered Rozalinda!"

Everyone's eyes swivelled back to Jonathan and my heart died within me. He said quietly. "Miles was sending the anonymous letters to Rozalinda. Blackmailing letters."

"You're lying Crown!"

Phil jerked Miles' arm painfully upwards. "I couldn't care less what Crown has done, but you'll pay for what you did to Jennifer! Either now or later!"

Almost as a reflex action Tom had seized Miles' other arm.

He glared at both of them, his eyes wild. "You're all against me! The police won't be! They'll listen to me! You'll all pay for this!"

"Shut your mouth," Tom said crudely.

"No wonder you could assure Harold they'd stop. Getting cold feet about your film part were you?" Phil asked through clenched teeth.

"Why?" Aunt Harriet asked, her eyes never leaving Jonathan's.

He said simply. "It was Rozalinda who killed Nanette and Sarah. She'd left Phil's party to meet someone. She'd been drinking and it was dark ... Then she came back to the party and behaved as if nothing had happened. Minutes later Jenny left for home, swerved to avoid the bodies in the road, was badly concussed and believed, like everyone else, that she had done it. Miles was jealous that Rozalinda was beginning an affair with someone else. He had been following her. He knew she'd done it all along."

"*Oh God,*" Tom's face was indescribable.

Phil said blankly. "So that's why she left so early. She was miles away by the time the police began questioning Jenny. And so was her car."

"And then *he* came," Miles burst out. "He found out and he murdered her!"

We sat in a shocked little group. Miles triumphant. Phil still coming to grips with what had been said. Tom stricken. Aunt Harriet believing. Jonathan and myself knelt on the floor, my body cradled against his. I scarcely noticed Mary, standing by Tom's side like a sleepwalker.

Aunt Harriet gave a deep, shuddering sigh. "Poor, frightened child. Causing all this heartache and tragedy. I'm glad, for your sake Jenny, that we know the truth. And I'm sure, under the circumstances, that the courts will show compassion to Jonathan."

"There's just one thing more," Jonathan said, his arm tightening round me.

Even Miles listened.

"I didn't kill Rozalinda. I knew nothing at all until I came here tonight to make sure Jenny was safe."

The room swam and then Mary stepped forward into the light.

"I wouldn't have let them arrest you, Jonathan."

"Sit down Mary," Tom said gently. "There's nothing you can do to help."

"There is," she looked at him with an expression of surprise. "You see, I killed her."

Twenty

There was complete silence. Mary's face and voice showed no expression. She stood in front of Aunt Harriet, a short, dumpy figure with a woollen dressing gown hastily tied around her waist and said:– "She made Tom love her."

"No!" Tom said. "No!" and leapt to his feet towards her. She shook her head. Refusing to be drawn into his arms.

"I knew there was something wrong. We weren't happy like we used to be. Not after the party. He ..." for the first time emotion entered her voice, choking it. "He didn't make love to me like he used to. Then we came here and it got worse. It was as if I didn't exist."

Tom gave a deep groan and buried his face in his hands, sinking back in his chair.

"Harold had gone to Oporto and Tom had said he was going out for a ride before dinner. I came in the villa to talk to Rozalinda and I heard them ..."

"Oh my God," Tom's face was ashen. "It didn't mean anything Mary. It ..."

The flat voice went remorselessly on. "I went back to our villa and waited for him. He didn't even speak to me. He was whistling and when I went in the bathroom after him I saw myself in the mirror and it was then that I hated her. I've never been pretty. I couldn't believe it when Tom said he loved me. Now I've had the children and my body ..." unknowingly she passed a hand across her stomach, "my body isn't even firm anymore. Rozalinda had everything. Money. A husband who worshipped her. Fame. Beauty. Why did she want my Tom as well? She could have had any man she wanted. All I wanted was Tom."

She gazed slowly round at our horrified eyes, at her husband's tear streaked face.

"The maid was on her way home. I gave her a letter to leave at Rozalinda's. I wrote that I knew what was in the other letters she had received. I didn't, but I knew they frightened her. And I wanted to frighten her. Then I went over to the villa and took the gun from Harold's desk. I wasn't going to kill her." Her voice held a compelling naivety. "She was in bed. I told her I knew she was having an affair with Tom and that he didn't love me anymore. She laughed at me." Her voice thickened. "She told me that I could have him back anytime I wanted and that I was being silly. She told me to put the gun down because it was loaded. And then she said," and the staring eyes were bright with tears. "She said she didn't want him anyway ... she said that he was a bore. That he was a lousy lover, only that wasn't the word she used and then she looked at me and she stopped laughing and said 'For God's sake put that thing down. You're not well Mary. It was nothing I tell you ...' but I just kept looking at her. At how beautiful she was and how hideous inside. There was a mirror in the ceiling above the bed and I thought of her and Tom ... and then she said that if I shot her no-one would ever know about Jenny ... her hands were shaking and there was sweat on her forehead. I was just staring at her, that was all. She was speaking quickly. So quickly I could hardly hear. She said that if I killed her no-one would ever know Jenny was innocent. That someone had found out and she would have to tell. I didn't know what she was talking about. I only knew that Tom would never look at me in the way he looked at her ... She said that she had run down Nanette and Sarah and been so frightened that she hadn't stopped and now someone had found out ..." Her glazed eyes focused with difficulty on Aunt Harriet. "Then I understood and I thought of Nanette and little Sarah and how she'd left them in the road not even knowing they were dead. And of Jenny and her injuries, and the trial and her face in all the papers and of how she has never been the same since. And Jonathan. And of how Jonathan wouldn't marry Jenny any more and of how he had called her filthy and a bitch and a murderess, and of how Jenny loved him. And of what she had done to my Tom. And I squeezed the trigger."

No-one moved or spoke. Outside the birds were beginning to sing in the woods, the first rays of early morning light seeping through the shutters.

Tom, looking ten years older than he had when he entered the room walked slowly across to his wife and put his arm around her shoulders. Silently she laid her head against him, and without speaking he led her across the room and out into the pale light. The door swung shut behind them. We remained motionless, staring at the empty spot where Mary had stood. It was Miles who moved first. No-one attempted to stop him. There was a smirk on his face.

"What chance now you telling the police about me?" and as no-one answered he laughed with genuine amusement and slammed the door behind him.

At last Aunt Harriet said wearily. "You'd better get dressed Jenny. You'll catch a chill."

Jonathan helped me to my feet, holding me close to him, oblivious of Aunt Harriet and Phil.

Safe in his arms, his heart thudding against mine, I had no wish to move. He said gently:– "It will be all right Jenny. Trust me."

"Yes," I said, "I always will."

Drained of emotion I went slowly upstairs to dress.

Mary a killer. It wasn't possible. Yet she had done it. Not one of us had doubted her. What would happen to her? And to the children? The shock that had enveloped us all, making us temporarily numb, was beginning to fade by the time I went back downstairs. My new feeling was one of steely determination. Whatever happened, Mary wasn't going to be punished for Rozalinda's death. She hadn't meant to kill her. Rozalinda had provoked her beyond all bearing. If she hadn't told her about Nanette and Sarah, Mary would never have shot her. I knew it. I had no need to convince anyone else. Aunt Harriet was saying:–

"I think what Jonathan suggests is the best ..."

"What's that?"

They were sitting in the kitchen. The colour was beginning to return to Aunt Harriet's cheeks, and Phil, like Jonathan, looked full of purpose.

"That we don't tell the police what happened. We let them get on with their enquiries and if they come to a verdict of suicide we leave it at that."

"Do you think they will?"

"When they find only Rozalinda's fingerprints on the gun, yes."

I stared at the three of them bewildered.

"But Mary killed her ... it will be Mary's fingerprints on the gun ..."

Aunt Harriet sighed. "When I went in that room, Jenny. I didn't know who had killed her. I thought at first it was Harold. I knew it was one of us and Rozalinda was already dead and I couldn't bear the thought of more suffering ..."

Phil, with fond exasperation said:– "While we were bringing Harold downstairs, Aunt Harriet wiped the gun and pressed Rozalinda's fingers around it, leaving it in her hand. That's where the police found it."

"But it could have been anyone! It could have been Miles!"

"I know dear, but I didn't have time to think. Only time to act. Besides, I knew that Rozalinda had been out somewhere the night of Phil's party. There were raindrops in her hair when she kissed me goodbye ... and since then she's been nervous and frightened. It would have been unnatural not to have wondered. I just couldn't bring myself to believe Rozalinda could have been so ..." she faltered. "So *treacherous.*"

"No wonder she paid all the clinic fees," Phil said brutally. "And you thought it was because she loved you."

I remembered her vibrant beauty, the way she had clasped me in her arms when I had arrived at the enclave. Kissing me on the cheek. A Judas kiss, not a kiss of love. Then I remembered how frightened she had been. How sorry. I said:– "She did love me in her way."

"You have a more forgiving heart than I have."

"And I'm glad," Jonathan said, pulling me down on his knee. "Which is one reason I'm marrying Jenny and not you, Phil."

Phil smiled wryly. "I don't think I'm the marrying kind. I'll go over to the Farrar's and tell them what we're doing.

We don't want Mary going to Harold and confessing again."

"No," Aunt Harriet stood up briskly. "And it's nearly seven. The police will be back soon and we have to get that key put back on the inside of the room. Mary must still have it."

"How come Harold wasn't here?" I asked.

"The sleeping tablets knocked him cold." Aunt Harriet said. "Though even if he knew I think he would go along with us. If there was a trial everything would come out. He wouldn't want that."

"And as it is," Jonathan said to me. "He'll never know what she was really like. It's better this way."

"Yes," I said fervently. "Much better."

Aunt Harriet was already scurrying down the garden path towards the Farrar's villa. Phil paused at the door, his eyes meeting mine. They were rueful but certainly not heartbroken. "Congratulations." he said.

Twenty-One

It was early autumn, and the sun slanted deep gold over the sea and the sand. The villas were boarded up, awaiting the arrival of their new occupants in the spring. No hint of the tragedy that had been enacted in them lingered. We stood on top of the dunes, gazing at the deserted beach and the giant breakers as they ploughed their way shorewards.

Jonathan lifted my left hand to his lips, the gold ring shining brightly. I moved closer, warm in the circle of his arms.

"Mary's new baby will be born in the spring. We did the right thing, Jenny."

"And ours in the summer."

I raised my lips for his kiss. Then, my head on his chest, I said:– "We must be back for the fifteenth. Phil has his first London concert."

"And Aunt Harriet is hoping to win the flower show at the summer fete."

I smiled. "And our holiday will be over."

"Oliveira has asked us to bring the baby next year."

"We will. But we won't leave Vigo and Spain to travel south. All the ghosts have been laid."

"I'm glad." He lifted my face to his. "I love you, Jenny Wren. God, how I love you."

And then he seized my hand and began to run down the dunes to the beach.

"What is it? I thought we were going back?" I protested laughing.

"Not yet." And he pulled me down beside him against the sheltered bank where we had first made love.

"Some things haven't changed, Jenny Wren!" and in the passion of his lovemaking, all the pain of the past was finally buried.